Joe R. Lansdale

This special signed
edition is limited to
1250 numbered copies.

This is copy __1135__.

The Events
Concerning

The Events Concerning

_____

Joe R. Lansdale

SUBTERRANEAN PRESS 2022

Signed, Limited Edition

ISBN
978-1-64524-100-3

Subterranean Press
PO Box 190106
Burton, MI 48519

subterraneanpress.com

Manufactured in the United States of America

In memory of Chris Mini, friend and reader.

Table of Contents:

Introduction

O NCE UPON A TIME WHEN I was a young man, not a kid, but young enough, I put together an anthology of my early stories. I titled it *Stories by Mama Lansdale's Youngest Boy.*

It was to be my first short story collection. As fate would have it, the publisher at the time was having difficulty getting to it, and gave me an out. I put it aside, and by that time, By Bizarre Hands appeared, *Stories* was set to arrive in second place and from a different publisher, Pulphouse. That happened, and then a New York publisher, Berkley Books, now defunct, picked it up with the proviso that I needed to add an original story or two for their publication.

Instead of two, I wrote one long one. "The Events Concerning a Nude Fold-Out Found in a Harlequin Romance." I didn't write it for Berkley directly, but for another publication edited by my wife and me, *Dark at Heart*, published by Dark Harvest. Another publishing house that has gone the way of fresh dinosaur turds.

The story received a Bram Stoker award, and the collection, which was now titled after one of the stories inside, "Bestsellers Guaranteed," came out with a dragon on the cover. They told me it was because dragons sold books.

Joe R. Lansdale

I didn't buy the premise that dragons sold books. I told them I bet it was because it was a cover they had already commissioned and could use cheaply by applying it to my book, without so much as the vaguest connection or concern.

This, in fact, turned out to be the case.

I was glad the book was published, but a cute dragon cover did me no favors because not only did I not buy the idea that dragons sold books, the public felt the same.

But, like much in publishing and film, and so on, it is now congealed blood stuck under the bridge.

Anyway, I thought for years I would write more about the characters in "The Events" story, but the years didn't think so. They passed without me hearing so much as a sigh from the detective team.

I had pretty much decided it would never happen. I assumed they had gone to seed. But then Bill Schafer at Subterranean suggested I see what else those folks were doing so many years ago.

I mentally drove a time train back to the year in which the first story occurred, and continued shortly thereafter with this tale. It was a story lying there waiting for me to pick it up.

It was fun to revisit the gang. They are a bit lighter hearted and less violent than some things I've written, though what they deal with here is no less nefarious, and may be even darker at the core than many of my other stories.

Perhaps, "The Events Concerning the One-Legged Dog With the Delicate Condition" will someday be written, a third tale about the gang. Can't say for sure, but I never say never.

The Events Concerning a Nude Fold-Out Found in a Harlequin Romance

LOOKING BACK ON IT, I wouldn't have thought something as strange as all this, full of the real coincidence of life, would have begun with a bad circus, but that's how it started, at least for me.

My luck had gone from bad to worse, then over the lip of worse, and into whatever lower level it can descend into. My job at the aluminum chair plant had played out and no rich relatives had died and left me any money. Fact was, I don't think the Cooks, least any that are kin to me, have any money, outside of a few quarters to put in a jukebox come Saturday night, maybe a few bucks to waste on something like pretzels and beer.

Me, I didn't even have money for beer or jukeboxes. I was collecting a little money on unemployment, and I was out beating the bushes for a job, but there didn't seem to be much in the way of work in Mud Creek. I couldn't even get on at the feed store carrying out bags of fertilizer and seed. All the sixteen-year-olds had that job.

It looked like I was going to have to move out of Mud Creek to find work, and though the idea of that didn't hurt my feelings any, there was Jasmine, my teenage daughter, and she still had a year of high school to finish before she went off to Nacogdoches to start her degree in anthropology at Stephen F. Austin State University, and I planned to follow her over there and find a place of my own where we could be near, and improve our relationship, which overall was all right to begin with. I just wanted more time with her.

Right then Jasmine lived with her mother, and her mother doesn't care a damn for me. She wanted to marry a guy that was going to be a high roller, and believe me, I wanted to be a high roller, but what she got was a guy who each time at the mark throws craps. No matter what I do, it turns to shit. Last break I felt I'd had in life was when I was ten and fell down and cracked my ankle. Well, maybe there was one good break after all. One that wasn't a bone. Jasmine. She's smart and pretty and ambitious and the love of my life.

But my marital problems and life's woes are not what this is about. I was saying about the circus.

It was mid-June, and I'd tried a couple places, looking for work, and hadn't gotten any, and I'd gone over to the employment office to talk to the people there and embarrass myself about not finding any work yet. They told me they didn't have anything for me either, but they didn't look embarrassed at all. When it's you and the employment office, better known as the unemployment office, feeling embarrassed is a one-way street and you're the one driving on it. They seem almost proud to tell you how many unemployment checks you got left, so it can kind of hang over your head like an anvil or something.

So, I thanked them like I meant it and went home, and believe me, that's no treat.

Home is a little apartment about the size of a washroom at a Fina Station, only not as nice and without the air-conditioning. The

The Events Concerning a Nude Fold-Out Found in a Harlequin Romance

window looks out over Main Street, and when a car drives by the window shakes, which is one of the reasons I leave it open most of the time. That and the fact I can hope for some sort of breeze to stir the dead, hot air around. The place is over a used bookstore called MARTHA'S BOOKS, and Martha is an all right lady if you like them mean. She's grumpy, about five hundred years old, weighs two-fifty when she's at her wrestling weight, wears men's clothing and has a bad leg and a faint black mustache to match the black wool ski cap she wears summer or winter, on account of her head is as bald as a river stone. I figure the cap is a funny sort of vanity, considering she doesn't do anything to get rid of that mustache. Still, she always does her nails in pink polish and she smokes those long feminine cigarettes that some women like, maybe thinking if the weeds look elegant enough they won't give them cancer.

Another thing about Martha, is with that bad leg she has a limp, and she helps that along with a golf putter she uses as a cane, putter-side up for a handle. See her coming down the street, which isn't often, you got to think there's not much you could add to make her any more gaudy, unless it's an assful of bright tail feathers and maybe some guys to follow her playing percussion instruments.

I liked to go down to Martha's from time to time and browse the books, and if I had a little spare change, I'd try to actually buy something now and then, or get something for Jasmine. I was especially fond of detective books, and Jasmine, bless her little heart, liked Harlequin Romances. She'd read them four or five a weekend when she wasn't dating boys, and since she was dating quite regularly now, she'd cut back mostly to one or two Harlequins a weekend. Still, that was too many. I kept hoping she'd outgrow it. The romance novels and the dates. I was scared to death she'd fall in love with some cowboy with a cheek full of snuff and end up ironing Western shirts and wiping baby asses before she was old enough to vote.

Anyway, after I didn't find any jobs and nobody died and left me any money, I went home and brooded, then went downstairs to Martha's to look for a book.

Jasmine had made out a list of the titles she was looking to collect, and I took the list with me just in case I came across something she needed. I thought if I did, I might buy it and get her a detective book too, or something like that, give it to her with the romance and maybe she'd read it. I'd done that several times, and so far, to the best of my knowledge, she hadn't read any of the non-romance novels. The others might as well have been used to level a vibrating refrigerator, but I kept on trying.

The stairs went down from my place and out into the street, and at the bottom, to the left of them, was Martha's. The store was in front and she lived in back. During business hours in the summer the door was always open since Martha wouldn't have put air conditioning in there if half the store had been a meat locker hung with prize beef. She was too cheap for that. She liked her mustache sweat-beaded, her bald head pink beneath her cap. The place smelled of books and faintly of boiled cabbage, or maybe that was some soured clothing somewhere. The two smells have always seemed a lot alike to me. It's the only place I know hotter and filthier than my apartment, but it does have the books. Lots of them.

I went in, and there on the wall was a flyer for a circus at three o'clock that day. Martha had this old post board just inside the door, and she'd let people pin up flyers if they wanted, and sometimes she'd leave them there a whole day before she tore them down and wrote out the day's receipts on the back of them with a stubby, tongue-licked pencil. I think that's the only reason she had the post board and let people put up flyers, so she'd have scratch paper.

The flyer was for a circus called THE JIM DANDY THREE RING CIRCUS, and that should have clued me, but it didn't. Truth is, I've never liked circuses. They depress me. Something about the animals and the people who work there strike me as desperate, as if they're living on the edge of a cliff and the cliff is about to break off. But I saw this flyer and I thought of Jasmine.

When she was little she loved circuses. Her mother and I used to take her, and I remembered the whole thing rather fondly. Jasmine would laugh so hard at the clowns you had to tell her to shut up, and she'd put her hands over her eyes and peek through her fingers at the wild animal acts.

Back then, things were pretty good, and I think her mother even liked me, and truth to tell, I thought I was a pretty good guy myself. I thought I had the world by the tail. It took me a few years to realize the closest I was to having the world by the tail was being a dingle berry on one of its ass hairs. These days, I felt like the most worthless sonofabitch that had ever squatted to shit over a pair of shoes. I guess it isn't hip or politically correct, but to me, a man without a job is like a man without balls.

Thinking about my problems also added to me wanting to go to the circus. Not only would I get a chance to be with Jasmine, it would help me get my mind off my troubles.

I got out my wallet and opened it and saw a few sad bills in there, but it looked to me that I had enough for the circus, and maybe I could even spring for dinner afterwards, if Jasmine was in the mood for a hot dog and a soda pop. She wanted anything more than that, she had to buy me dinner, and I'd let her, since the money came from her mother, my darling ex-wife, Connie—may she grow like an onion with her head in the ground.

Mommy Dearest didn't seem to be shy of the bucks these days on account of she was letting old Gerald the Oil Man drop his drill down her oil shaft on a nightly basis.

Not that I'm bitter about it or anything. Him banging my ex-wife and being built like Tarzan and not losing any of his hair at the age of forty didn't bother me a bit.

I put my wallet away and turned and saw Martha behind the counter looking at me. She twisted on the stool and said, "Got a job yet?"

I just love a small town. You fart and everyone looks in your direction and starts fanning.

"No, not yet," I said.

"You looking for some kind of a career?"

"I'm looking for work."

"Any kind of work?"

"Right now, yes. You got something for me?"

"Naw. Can't pay my rent as it is."

"You're just curious, then?"

"Yeah. You want to go to that circus?"

"I don't know. Maybe. Is this a trick question too?"

"Guy put up the flyer gave me a couple tickets for letting him have the space on the board there. I'd give them to you for stacking some books. I don't really want to do it."

"Stack the books or give me the tickets?"

"Neither one. But you stack them Harlequins for me, I'll give you the tickets."

I looked at my wrist where my watch used to be before I pawned it. "You got the time?"

She looked at her watch. "Two o'clock."

"I like the deal," I said, "but the circus starts at three and I wanted to take my daughter."

Martha shook out one of her delicate little cigarettes and lit it, studied me. It made me feel funny. Like I was a shit smear on a laboratory slide. Most I'd ever talked to her before was when I asked where the new detective novels were and she grumped around and finally told me, as if it was a secret she'd rather have kept.

"Tell you what," Martha said, "I'll give you the tickets now, and you come back tomorrow morning and put up the books for me."

"That's nice of you," I said.

"Not really. I know where you live, and you don't come put up my romance novels tomorrow, I'll hunt you down and kill you."

I looked for a smile, but I didn't see any.

"That's one way to do business," I said.

"The only way. Here." She opened a drawer and pulled out the tickets and I went over and took them. "By the way, what's your name, boy? See you in here all the time, but don't know your name."

Boy? Was she talking to me?

"Plebin Cook," I said. "And I've always assumed you're Martha."

"Martha ain't much of a name, but it beats Plebin. Plebin's awful. I was named that I'd get it changed. Call yourself most anything and it'd be better than Plebin."

"I'll tell my poor, old, gray-haired mother what you said."

"You must have been an accident and that's why she named you that. You got an older brother or sister?"

"A brother."

"How much older?"

Earning these tickets was getting to be painful. "Sixteen years."

"What's his name?"

"Jim."

"There you are. You were an accident. Jim's a normal name. Her naming you Plebin is unconscious revenge. I read about stuff like that in one of those psychology books came in. Called KNOW WHY THINGS HAPPEN TO YOU. You ought to read it. Thing it'd tell you is to get your name changed to something normal. Right name will give you a whole nuther outlook about yourself."

I had a vision of shoving those circus tickets down her throat, but I restrained myself for Jasmine's sake. "No joke? Well, I'll see you tomorrow."

"Eight o'clock sharp. Go stacking 'em after nine, gets so hot in here you'll faint. A Yankee visiting some relatives came in here and did just that. Found him about closing time over there by the historicals and the Gothic Romances. Had to call an ambulance to come get him. Got out of here with one of my Gothics clutched in his hand. Didn't pay me a cent for it."

"And people think a job like this is pretty easy."

"They just don't know," Martha said.

I said thanks and goodbye and started to turn away.

"Hey," Martha said. "You decide to get your name changed, they'll do stuff like that for you over at the court house."

"I'll keep that in mind," I said.

The Events Concerning a Nude Fold-Out
Found in a Harlequin Romance

I DIDN'T WANT any more of Martha, so I went over to the drugstore and used the payphone there and called Jasmine. Her mother answered.

"Hi, Connie," I said.

"Get a job yet?"

"No," I said. "But I'm closing in on some prospects."

"Bet you are. What do you want?"

"Jasmine in?"

"You want to talk to her?"

No, I thought. Just ask for the hell of it. But I said, "If I may."

The phone clattered on something hard, a little more violently than necessary, I thought. A moment later Jasmine came on the line. "Daddy."

"Hi, Baby Darling. Want to go to the circus?"

"The circus?"

"The Jim Dandy Circus is in town, and I've got tickets."

"Yeah. Really." She sounded as if I'd asked her if she wanted to have her teeth cleaned.

"You used to like the circuses."

"When I was ten."

"That was just seven years ago."

"That's a long time."

"Only when you're seventeen. Want to go or not? I'll even spring for a hot dog."

"You know what they make hot dogs out of?"

"I try not to think about it. I figure I get some chili on it, whatever's in the dog dies."

"Guess you want me to come by and get you?"

"That would be nice. Circus starts at three. That's less than an hour away."

"All right, but Daddy?"

"Yeah."

"Don't call me Baby Darling in public. Someone could hear."

"We can't have that."

"Really, Daddy. I'm getting to be a woman now. It's… I don't know…kind of…"

"Hokey?"

"That's it."

"Gotcha."

THE CIRCUS WAS not under the big top, but was inside the Mud Creek Exhibition center, which Mud Creek needs about as much as I need a second dick. I don't use the first one as it is. Oh, I pee out of it, but you know what I mean.

The circus was weak from the start, but Jasmine seemed to have a pretty good time, even if the performing bears were so goddamned old I thought we were going to have to go down there and help them out of their cages. The tiger act was scary, because it looked as if the tigers were definitely in control, but the overweight Ringmaster got out alive, and the elephants came on, so old and wrinkled they looked like drunks in baggy pants. That was the best of it. After that, the dog act, conducted by Waldo the Great, got out of hand, and his performing poodles went X-rated, and the real doo-doo hit the fan.

Idiot trainer had apparently put one of the bitches to work while she was in heat, and in response, the male dogs jumped her and started poking, the biggest male finally winning the honors and the other five running about as if their brains had rolled out of their ears.

Waldo the Great went a little nuts and started kicking the forni-
cating dogs, but they wouldn't let up. The male dog kept his goober
in the slot even when Waldo's kicks made his hind legs leave the
ground. He didn't even yip.

I heard a kid behind us say, "Mommy, what are the puppies
doing?"

And Mommy, not missing a beat, said, "They're doing a trick,
dear."

Children were screaming. Waldo began kicking at the remain-
ing dogs indiscriminately, and they darted for cover. Members of the
circus rushed Waldo the Great. There were disappointed and injured
dogs hunching and yipping all over the place. Waldo went back to the
horny male and tried once more to discourage him. He really put the
boot to him, but the ole boy really hung in there. I was kind of proud
of him. One of the other dogs, innocent, except for confusion, and a
gyrating ass and a dick like a rolled-back lipstick tube, made an error in
geography and humped air past Waldo and got a kick in the ass for it.

He sailed way up and into the bleachers, went so high his fleas
should have served cocktails and dinner on him. Came down like
a bomb, hit between a crack in the bleachers with a yip. I didn't see
him come out from under there. He didn't yip again.

The little boy behind me said, "Is that a trick too?"

"Yes," Mommy said. "It doesn't hurt him. He knows how to land."

I certainly hoped so.

Not everyone took it as casually as Mommy. Some dog lovers
came out of the bleachers and there was a fight. Couple of cowboys
started trying to do to Waldo what he had done to the poodles.

Meanwhile, back at the ranch, so to speak, the two amorous
mutts were still at it, the male laying pipe like there was no tomorrow.

Yes sir, a pleasant afternoon trip to the circus with my daughter. Another debacle. It was merely typical of the luck I had been experiencing. Even a free ticket to the circus could turn to shit.

Jasmine and I left while a cowboy down from the bleachers was using Waldo the Great as a punching bag. One of the ungrateful poodles was biting the cowboy on the boot.

ME AND JASMINE didn't have hot dogs. We ended up at a Mexican place, and Jasmine paid for it. Halfway through the meal Jasmine looked up at me and frowned.

"Daddy, I can always count on you for a good time."

"Hey," I said, "what were you expecting for free tickets? Goddamn Ringling Brothers?"

"Really, Daddy. I enjoyed it. Weirdness follows you around. At Mom's there isn't anything to do but watch television, and Mom and Gerald always go to bed about nine o'clock, so they're no fun."

"I guess not," I said, thinking nine o'clock was awful early to be sleepy. I hoped the sonofabitch gave her the clap.

After dinner, Jasmine dropped me off and next morning I went down to Martha's and she grunted at me and showed me the Harlequins and where they needed to go, in alphabetical order, so I started in placing them. After about an hour of that, it got hot and I had to stop and talk Martha into letting me go over to the drugstore and buy a Coke.

When I came back with it, there was a guy in there with a box of Harlequin Romances. He was tall and lean and not bad-looking, except that he had one of those little pencil-line mustaches that looked as if he'd missed a spot shaving or had a stain line from sipping chocolate milk. Except for a black eye, his face was oddly unlined, as if little that happened to him in life found representation there. I thought he looked familiar. A moment later, it came to me. He was the guy at the circus with the performing dogs. I hadn't recognized him without his gold lamé tights. I could picture him clearly now, his foot up in the air, a poodle being launched from it. Waldo the Great.

He had a box of books on the desk in front of Martha. All Harlequin Romances. He reached out and ran his fingers over the spines. "I really hate to get rid of these," he was saying to Martha, and his voice was as sweet as a cooing turtle dove. "Really hate it, but see, I'm currently unemployed and extra finances, even of a small nature, are needed, and considering all the books I read, well, they're outgrowing my trailer. I tell you, it hurts me to dispense with these. Just seeing them on my shelves cheers me... Oh, I take these books so to heart. If life could be like these, oh what a life that would be. But somebody always messes it up." He touched the books. "True love. Romance. Happy endings. Oh, it should be that way, you know. We live such a miserable existence. We—"

"Hey," Martha said. "Actually, I don't give a shit why you want to get rid of them. And if life was like a Harlequin Romance, I'd put a gun in my mouth. You want to sell this crap, or not?"

Martha always tries to endear herself to her customers. I reckon she's got a trust fund somewhere and her mission on earth is to make as many people miserable as possible. Still, that seemed blunt even for her.

"Well, now," Waldo said. "I was merely expressing a heartfelt opinion. Nothing more. I could take my trade elsewhere."

"No skin off my rosy red ass," Martha said. "You want, that man over there will help you carry this shit back out to the car."

He looked at me. I blushed, nodded, drank more of my Coke.

He looked back at Martha. "Very well. I'll sell them to you, but only because I'm pressed to rid myself of them. Otherwise, I wouldn't take twice what you want to give for them."

"For you, Mister Asshole," Martha said, "just for you, I'll give you half of what I normally offer. Take it or leave it."

Waldo, Mr. Asshole, paused for a moment, studying Martha. I could see the side of his face, and just below his blackened eye there was a twitch, just once, then his face was smooth again.

"All right, let's conduct our business and get it over with," he said.

Martha counted the books, opened the cash register and gave Waldo a handful of bills. "Against my better judgment, there's the whole price."

"What in the world did I ever do to you?" Waldo the Great, alias, Mr. Asshole, said. He almost looked really hurt. It was hard to tell. I'd never seen a face like that. So smooth. So expressionless. It was disconcerting.

"You breathe," Martha said, "that's enough of an offense." With that, Waldo, Mr. Asshole, went out of the store, head up, back straight.

"Friend of yours?" I asked.

"Yeah," Martha said. "Me and him are fuckin'."

"I thought the two of you were pretty warm."

"I don't know. I really can't believe it happened like that."

"You weren't as sweet as usual."

"Can't explain it. One of those things. Ever had that happen? Meet someone right off, and you just don't like them, and you don't know why."

"I always just shoot them. Saves a lot of breath."

She ignored me. "Like it's chemistry or something. That guy came in here, it was like someone drove by and tossed a rattlesnake through the door. I didn't like him on sight. Sometimes I think that there's certain people that are predators, and the rest of us, we pick up on it, even if it isn't obvious through their actions, and we react to it. And maybe I'm an asshole."

"That's a possibility," I said. "You being an asshole, I mean. But I got to tell you, I don't like him much either. Kind of makes my skin crawl, that unlined face and all."

I told her about the circus and the dogs.

"That doesn't surprise me any," Martha said. "I mean, anyone can lose their cool. I've kicked a dog in my time—"

"I find that hard to believe."

"—but I tell you, that guy hasn't got all the corn on his cob. I can sense it. Here, put these up. Earn your goddamn circus tickets."

I finished off the Coke, got the box of Harlequins Waldo had brought in, took them over to the romance section and put them on the floor.

I pulled one out to look at the author's name, and something fell out of the book. It was a folded piece of paper. I picked it up and unfolded it. It was a magazine fold-out of a naked woman, sort you see in the cheaper tits and ass magazines. She had breasts just a little smaller than watermelons and she was grabbing her ankles, holding her legs in a spread eagle position, as if waiting for some unsuspecting traveler to fall in. There were thick black paint lines slashed at the neck, torso, elbows, wrist, waist, knees and ankles. The eyes had been blackened with the marker so that they looked like nothing more than enormous skull sockets. A circle had been drawn around her vagina and there was a big black dot dead center of it, like a bullseye. I turned it over. On the back over the printing there was written in black with a firm hand: *Nothing really hooks together. Life lacks romance.*

Looking at the photograph and those lines made me feel peculiar. I refolded the fold-out and started to replace it inside the book, then I thought maybe I'd throw it in the trash, but finally decided to keep it out of curiosity.

I shoved it into my back pocket and finished putting up the books, then got ready to leave. As I was going, Martha said, "You want a job here putting up books I'll take you on half a day five days a week. Monday through Friday. Saves some wear on my bad leg. I can pay you a little. Won't be much, but I don't figure you're worth much to me."

"That's a sweet offer, Martha, but I don't know."

"You say you want work."

"I do, but half a day isn't enough."

"More than you're working now, and I'll pay in cash. No taxes, no bullshit with the employment office."

"All right," I said. "You got a deal."

"Start tomorrow."

༠

I WAS LYING naked on the bed with just the nightlight on reading a hard-boiled mystery novel. The window was open as always and there was actually a pretty nice breeze blowing in. I felt like I used to when I was twelve and staying up late and reading with a flashlight under the covers and a cool spring wind was blowing in through the window screen, and Mom and Dad were in the next room and I was loved and protected and was going to live forever. Pleasant.

There was a knock at the door.

That figured.

I got up and pulled on my pajama bottoms and put on a robe and went to the door. It was Jasmine. She had her long, dark hair tied back in a pony tail and she was wearing jeans and a shirt buttoned up wrong. She had a suitcase in her hand.

"Connie again?"

"Her and that man," Jasmine said as she came inside. "I hate them."

"You don't hate your mother. She's an asshole, but you don't hate her."

"You hate her."

"That's different."

"Can I stay here for a while?"

"Sure. There's almost enough room for me, so I'm sure you'll find it cozy."

"You're not glad to see me?"

"I'm glad to see you. I'm always glad to see you. But this won't work out. Look how small this place is. Besides, you've done this before. Couple times. You come here, eat all my cereal, start missing your comforts, and then you go home."

"Not this time."

"All right. Not this time. Hungry?"

"I really don't want any cereal."

"I actually have some lunch meat this time. It's not quite green."

"Sounds yummy."

I made a couple of sandwiches and poured us some slightly tainted milk and we talked a moment, then Jasmine saw the fold-out on the dresser and picked it up. I had pulled it from my pocket when I got home and tossed it there.

She opened it up and looked at it, then smiled at me. It was the same smile her mother used when she was turning on the charm, or was about to make me feel small enough to wear doll clothes.

"Daddy, dear!"

"I found it."

"Say you did?"

"Cut it out. It was in one of the books I was putting up today. I thought it was weird and I stuck it in my back pocket. I should have thrown it away."

Jasmine smiled at me, examined the fold-out closely. "Daddy, do men like women like this? That big, I mean?"

"Some do. Yes."

"Do you?"

"Of course not."

"What are these lines?"

"I don't know exactly, but that's what I thought was weird. It got my mind working overtime."

"You mean like the 'What If' game?"

The "What If" game was something Jasmine and I had made up when she was little, and had never really quit playing, though our opportunities to play it had decreased sharply over the last couple of years. It grew out of my thinking I was going to be a writer. I'd see something and I'd extrapolate. An example was an old car I saw once where someone had finger-written in the dust on the trunk lid: THERE'S A BODY IN THE TRUNK.

Well, I thought about that and tried to make a story of it. Say there was a body in the trunk. How did it get there? Is the woman driving the car aware it's there? Did she commit the murder? That sort of thing. Then I'd try to write a story. After fifty or so stories, and three times that many rejects, I gave up writing them, and Jasmine and I started kicking ideas like that back and forth, for fun. That way I could still feed my imagination, but I could quit kidding myself that I could write. Also, Jasmine got a kick out of it.

"Let's play, Daddy?"

"All right. I'll start. I saw those slashes on that fold-out, and I got to thinking, why are these lines drawn?"

"Because they look like cuts," Jasmine said. "You know, like a chart for how to butcher meat."

"That's what I thought. Then I thought, it's just a picture, and it could have been marked up without any real motive. Absentminded doodling. Or it could have been done by someone who didn't like women, and this was sort of an imaginary revenge. Turning women into meat in his mind. Dehumanizing them."

"Or it could be representative of what he's actually done or plans to do. Wow! Maybe we've got a real mystery here."

"My last real mystery was what finished your mom and me off."

That was the body in the trunk business. I didn't tell it all before. I got so into that scenario I called a friend of mine, Sam, down at the cop shop and got him geared up about there being a body in the trunk of a car. I told it good, with details I'd made up and didn't even know I'd made up. I really get into this stuff. The real and the unreal get a little hard for me to tell apart. Or it used to be that way. Not anymore.

Bottom line is Sam pursued the matter, and the only thing in the trunk was a spare tire. Sam was a little unhappy with me. The cop shop was a little unhappy with him. My wife, finally tired of my make-believe, kicked me out and went for the oil man. He didn't make up stories. He made money and had all his hair and was probably hung like a water buffalo.

"But say we knew the guy who marked this picture, Daddy. And say we started watching him, just to see—"

"We do know him. Kind of."

I told her about Waldo the Great and his books and Martha's reaction.

"That's even weirder," Jasmine said. "This bookstore lady—"

"Martha."

"—does she seem like a good judge of character?"

"She hates just about everybody, I think."

"Well, for 'What If's' sake, say she is a good judge of character. And this guy really is nuts. And he's done this kind of thing to a fold-out because…say…say…"

"He wants life to be like a Harlequin Romance. Only it isn't. Women don't always fit his image of what they should be—like the women in the books he reads."

"Oh, that's good, Daddy. Really. He's gone nuts, not because of violent films and movies, but because of a misguided view about romance. I love it."

"Makes as much sense as a guy saying he axed a family because he saw a horror movie or read a horror novel. There's got to be more to it than that, of course. Rotten childhood, genetic makeup. Most people who see or read horror novels, romance novels, whatever, get their thrills vicariously. It's a catharsis. But in the same way a horror movie or book might set someone off who's already messed up, someone wound-up and ready to spring, the Harlequins do it for our man. He has so little idea what real life is like, he expects it to be like the Harlequins, or desperately wants it to be that way, and when it isn't, his frustrations build, and—"

"He kills women, cuts them up, disposes of their bodies. It's delicious. Really delicious."

"It's silly. There's a sleeping bag in the closet. Get it out when you get sleepy. Me, I'm going to go to bed. I got a part-time job downstairs at Martha's, and I start tomorrow."

"That's great, Daddy. Mom said you'd never find a job."

On that note, I went to bed.

NEXT MORNING I went down to Martha's and started to work. She had a storeroom full of books. Some of them were stuck together with age, and some were full of worms. Being a fanatic book-lover, it hurt me, but I got rid of the bad ones in the dumpster out back, then loaded some boxes of good-condition books on a hand truck and wheeled them out and began putting them up in alphabetical order in their proper sections.

About nine that morning, Jasmine came down and I heard her say something to Martha, then she came around the corner of the detective section and smiled at me. She looked so much like her mother it hurt me. She had her hair pulled back and tied at her neck and she was starting to sweat. She wore white shorts, cut a little too short if you ask me, and a loose red T-shirt and sandals. She was carrying a yellow pad with a pencil.

"What you doing?" I asked.

"Figuring out what Waldo the Great's up to. I been working on it ever since I got up. I got lots of notes here."

"What'd you have for breakfast?"

"Same as you, I bet. A Coke."

"Right. It's important we pay attention to nutrition, Baby Darling."

"You want to hear about Waldo or not?"

"Yeah, tell me, what's he up to?"

"He's looking for a job."

"Because he got fired for the dog-kicking business?"

"Yeah. So, he's staying in the trailer park here, and he's looking for a job. Or maybe he's got some savings and he's just hanging out for a while before he moves on. Let's just say all that for 'What If's' sake."

"All right, now what?"

"Just for fun, to play the game all the way, let's go out to the trailer park and see if he's living there. If he is, we ought to be able to find him. He's got all these dogs, so there should be some signs of them, don't you think?"

"Wait a minute. You're not planning on checking?"

"Just for the 'What If' game."

"Like I said, he could have moved on."

"That's what we'll find out. Later, we can go over to the trailer park and look around, play detective."

"That's carrying it too far."

"Why? It's just a game. We don't have to bother him."

"I don't know. I don't think so."

"Why not?" It was Martha. She came around the corner of the bookshelves leaning on her golf putter. "It's just a game."

"Aren't you supposed to be counting your money, or something?" I said to Martha. "Kill some of those roaches in your storeroom. That club would be just the tool for it."

"I couldn't help but overhear you because I was leaning against the other side of the bookshelf listening," Martha said.

"That'll do it," I said, and shelved a Mickey Spillane.

"We've spoke, but I don't think we've actually met," Jasmine said to Martha. "I'm his daughter."

"Tough to admit, I'm sure," Martha said.

Jasmine and Martha smiled at each other and shook hands.

"Why don't we go over there tonight?" Martha said. "I need something to do."

"To the trailer park?" I asked.

"Of course," Martha said.

"Not likely," I said. "I've had it with the detective business, imaginary or otherwise. It'll be a cold day in hell when I have anything else to do with it, in any manner, shape or form. And you can take that to the bank."

❧

THAT NIGHT, PRESUMABLY an example of a cold day in hell, around nine-thirty, we drove over to the only trailer park in Mud Creek and looked around.

Waldo hadn't moved on. Being astute detectives, we found his trailer right away. It was bright blue and there was red lettering on the side that read: WALDO THE GREAT AND HIS MAGNIFICENT CANINES. The trailer was next to a big pickup with a trailer hitch and there were lights on in the trailer.

We were in Martha's old Dodge van, and we drove by Waldo's and around the loop in the park and out of there. Martha went a short distance, turned down a hard clay road that wound along the side of the creek and through a patch of woods and ended up at the rear of the trailer park, about even with Waldo's trailer. It was a bit of distance away, but you could see his trailer through the branches of the trees that surrounded the park. Martha parked to the side of the road and spoke to Jasmine. "Honey, hand me them binoculars out of the glove box."

Jasmine did just that.

"These suckers are infra-red," Martha said. "You can see a mole on a gnat's ass with one of these dead of night during a blizzard."

"And why in the world would you have a pair?" I asked.

"I used to do a little surveillance for a private investigation agency in Houston. I sort of borrowed these when I left. You know, boss I had hadn't been such a dick, I'd have stayed with that job. I was born to it."

"Sounds exciting," Jasmine said.

"It beat smelling book dust, I'll tell you that." Martha rolled down her window and put the glasses to her face and pointed them at Waldo's trailer.

"He's at the window," she said.

"This has gone far enough," I said. "We're not supposed to be doing this. It's an invasion of privacy."

"Settle down. He ain't got his pecker out or nothing," Martha said. "Wish he did, though. He's an asshole, but he ain't bad-looking. I wonder what kind of rod he's got on him?"

I looked at Jasmine. She looked a little stunned. "Listen here," I said. "My daughter's here."

"No shit," Martha said. "Listen, you stuffy old fart. She's grown up enough to know a man's got a hooter on him and what it looks like."

Jasmine's face was split by a weak smile. "Well, I know what they are, of course."

"All right, we're all versed in biology," I said. "Let's go. I've got a good book waiting at home."

"Hold the goddamn phone," Martha said. "He's coming out of the trailer."

I looked, and I could see Waldo's shape framed in the trailer's doorway. One of the poodles ran up behind him and he back-kicked it inside without even looking, went down the metal steps and closed and locked the trailer, got in his pickup and drove away.

"He's off," Martha said.

"Yeah. Probably to a fried chicken place," I said.

Martha lowered the binoculars and looked over her seat at me. "Would you quit fucking up the game? 'What If' is going on here."

"Yeah, Daddy," Jasmine said. "We're playing 'What If.'"

Martha cranked the van and followed the clay road as it curved around the park and out into the street. She went right. A moment later, we saw the back of Waldo's pickup. He had an arm hanging out the window and a cigarette was between his fingers and sparks were flaring off of it and flickering into the night.

"Smokey Bear'd come down on his ass like a ton of bricks, he seen that," Martha said.

We followed him to the end of the street and out onto the main drag, such as it is in Mud Creek. He pulled into a fried chicken joint.

"See," I said.

"Even murderers have to eat," Martha said, and she drove on by.

Joe R. Lansdale

MY PLAN WAS to end the business there, but it didn't work that way.
I pulled out of it and let them stay with it. All that week Martha
and Jasmine played "What If." They pinned up the fold-out in my
apartment and they wrote out scenarios for who Waldo was and
what he'd done, and so on. They drove out to his place at night and
discovered he kept weird hours, went out at all times of the night.
They discovered he let the poodles out for bathroom breaks twice
a night and that there was one less than there had been during the
circus act. I guess Mommy had been wrong when she told her kid
the poodle knew how to land.

It was kind of odd seeing Jasmine and Martha become friends
like that. Martha had struck me as having all the imagination of a
fencepost, but under that rough exterior and that loud mouth was a
rough exterior and a loud mouth with an imagination.

I also suspicioned that she had lied about not being able to pay
her rent. The store didn't make that much, but she always seemed
to have money. As far as the store went, it got so I was running
it by myself, fulltime, not only putting up books, but waiting on
customers and closing up at night. Martha paid me well enough for
it, however, so I didn't complain, but when she and Jasmine would
come down from my place talking about their "killer," etc., I felt a
little jealous. Jasmine had moved in with me, and now that I had my
daughter back, she spent all her time with a bald-headed, mustached
lady who was her father's boss.

Worse, Connie had been on my case about Jasmine and how
my only daughter was living in a shit hole and being exposed to bad
elements. The worst being me, of course. She came by the apartment a couple of times to tell me about it and to try and get Jasmine
to go home.

I told her Jasmine was free to go home anytime she chose, and Jasmine explained that she had no intention of going home. She liked her sleeping bag and Daddy let her have Coke for breakfast. I sort of wish she hadn't mentioned the Coke part. She'd only had that for breakfast one morning, but she knew it'd get her mother's goat, and it had. Only thing was, now Connie could hang another sword over my head. Failure to provide proper nutrition for my only child.

Anyway, I was working in the store one day—well, working on reading a detective novel—when Martha and Jasmine came in.

"Get your goddamn feet off my desk," Martha said.

"Glad to see you," I said, lowering my feet and putting a marker in the book.

"Get off my stool," Martha said. "Quit reading that damn book and put some up."

I got off the stool. "You two have a pleasant day, Massah Martha?"

"Eat shit, Plebin," Martha said, leaning her golf club against the counter and mounting her stool.

"Daddy, Martha and I have been snooping. Listen what we got. Martha had this idea to go over to the newspaper office in LaBorde and look at back issues—"

"LaBorde?" I said.

"Bigger town. Bigger paper," Martha said, sticking one of her dainty cigarettes into her mouth and lighting it.

"We went through some older papers," Jasmine said, "and since LaBorde covers a lot of the small towns around here, we found ads for the Jim Dandy Circus in several of them, and we were able to pinpoint on a map the route of the circus up to Mud Creek, and the latest paper showed Marvel Creek to be the next stop, and—"

"Slow down," I said. "What's the circus got to do with your so-called investigation?"

"You look at the papers and read about the towns where the circus showed up," Martha said, "and there's in every one of them something about a missing woman, or young girl. In a couple cases, bodies have been found. Sometimes they were found a week or so after the circus came to town, but most of the news articles indicate the missing women disappeared at the time of the circus."

"Of course, we determined this, not the papers," Jasmine said. "We made the connection between the circus and the bodies."

"In the case of the bodies, both were found after the circus passed through," Martha said, "but from the estimated times of death the papers gave, we've been able to figure they were killed about the time the circus was in town. And my guess is those missing women are dead too, and by the same hand."

"Waldo's?" I said.

"That's right," Martha said.

I considered all that.

Jasmine said, "Pretty coincidental, don't you think?"

"Well, yeah," I said, "but that doesn't mean—"

"And the two bodies had been mutilated," Martha said. She leaned against the counter and reached into her shirt pocket and pulled out the fold-out I had found. She smoothed it out on the counter top. "Body parts were missing. And I bet they were cut up, just like this fold-out is marked. As for the missing body parts, eyes and pussies, I figure. Those are the parts he has circled and blacked out."

"Watch your language," I said to Martha.

No one seemed to take much note of me.

"The bodies were found in the town's local dump," Jasmine said.

"It's curious," I admitted, "but still, to accuse a man of murder on the basis of circumstantial evidence."

"One more thing," Martha said. "Both bodies had traces of black paint on them. Like it had been used to mark the areas the killer wanted to cut, and I presume, did cut. That's certainly a lot of goddamn circumstantial evidence, isn't it?"

"Enough that we're going to keep an eye on Waldo," Jasmine said.

I MUST ADMIT right now that I didn't think even then, after what I had been told, there was anything to this Waldo the Great as murderer. It struck me that murders and disappearances happen all the time, and that if one were to look through the LaBorde paper carefully, it would be possible to discover there had been many of both, especially disappearances, before and after the arrival of the circus. I mean that paper covered a lot of small towns and communities, and LaBorde was a fairly large town itself. A small city actually. Most of the disappearances would turn out to be nothing more than someone leaving on a trip for a few days without telling anyone, and most of the murders would be committed by a friend or relative of the victim and would have nothing to do with the circus or marked-up fold-outs.

Of course, the fact that the two discovered bodies had been mutilated gave me pause, but not enough to go to the law about it. That was just the sort of half-baked idea that had gotten my ass in a crack earlier.

Still, that night, I went with Martha and Jasmine out to the trailer park.

It was cloudy that night and jags of lightning made occasional cuts through the cloud cover and thunder rumbled and light drops of rain fell on the windshield of Martha's van.

We drove out to the road behind the park about dark, peeked out the windows and through the gaps in the trees. The handful of pole lights in the park were gauzy in the wet night and sad as dying fireflies. Their poor, damp rays fell against some of the trees—their branches waving in the wind like the fluttering hands of distressed lunatics—and forced the beads of rain on the branches to give up tiny rainbows. The rainbows rose up, misted outward a small distance, then once beyond the small circumference of light, their beauty was consumed by the night.

Martha got out her binoculars and Jasmine sat on the front passenger side with a notepad and pen, ready to record anything Martha told her to. They felt that the more documentation they had, the easier it would be to convince the police that Waldo was a murderer.

I was in the seat behind theirs, my legs stretched out and my back against the van, looking away from the trailer most of the time, wondering how I had let myself in on this. About midnight I began to feel both sleepy and silly. I unwrapped a candy bar and ate it.

"Would you quit that goddamn smacking back there," Martha said. "It makes me nervous."

"Pardon me all to hell," I said, and wadded up the wrapper noisily and tossed it on the floorboard.

"Daddy, would you quit?" Jasmine said.

"Now we got something," Martha said.

I sat up and turned around. There were no lights on in the trailers in the park except for Waldo's trailer; a dirty, orange glow shone behind one of his windows, like a fresh slice of smoked cheese. Other than that, there was only the pole lights, and they didn't offer much. Just those little rainbows made of bad light and rain. Without the binoculars there was little to observe in detail, because it was a pretty good distance from where we were to Waldo's trailer, but I could see him coming out of the door, holding it open, the whole pack of poodles following after.

Waldo bent down by the trailer and pulled a small shovel out from beneath it. The poodles wandered around and started doing their bathroom business. Waldo cupped his hands over a cigarette and lit it with a lighter and smoked while he noted the dog's delivery spots. After a while he went about scooping up their messes with his shovel and making several trips to the dumpster to get rid of it.

Finished, he pushed the shovel beneath the trailer and smoked another cigarette and ground it hard beneath his heel and opened the trailer door and called to the dogs. They bounded up the steps and into the trailer like it was one of their circus tricks. No poodle tried to fuck another poodle. Waldo didn't kick anybody. He went inside, and a moment later came out again, this time minus the poodles. He was carrying something. A box. He looked about carefully, then placed the box in the back of his pickup. He went back inside the trailer.

"Goddamn," Martha said. "There's a woman's leg in that box."

"Let me see," I said.

"You can't see it now," she said. "It's down in the bed of the truck."

She gave me the binoculars anyway, and I looked. She was right. I couldn't see what was in the bed of the truck. "He wouldn't just put a woman's leg in the back of his pickup," I said.

"Well, he did," Martha said.

"Oh God," Jasmine said, and she flicked on her pen light and glanced at her watch and started writing on her notepad, talking aloud as she did. "Twelve-o-five, Waldo put woman's leg in the bed of his truck. Oh, shit, who do you think it could be?"

"One could hope it's that goddamn bitch down at the county clerk's office," Martha said. "I been waiting for something to happen to her."

"Martha!" Jasmine said.

"Just kidding," Martha said. "Kinda."

I had the binoculars tight against my face as the trailer door opened again. I could see very well with the infra-red business. Waldo came out with another box. As he came down the steps, the box tilted slightly. It was open at the top and I could see very clearly what was in it.

"A woman's head," I said. My voice sounded small and childish.

"Jesus Christ," Martha said. "I didn't really, really, believe he was a murderer."

Waldo was back inside the trailer. A moment later he reappeared. Smaller boxes under each arm.

"Let me see," Jasmine said.

"No," I said. "You don't need to."

"But…" Jasmine began.

"Listen to your father," Martha said.

I handed the binoculars back to Martha. She didn't look through them. We didn't need to try and see what was in the other boxes. We knew. The rest of Waldo's victim.

Waldo unfolded a tarp in the back of his pickup and stretched it across the truck bed and fastened it at all corners, then got inside the cab and cranked the engine.

"Do we go to the police now?" Jasmine said.

"After we find out where he's taking the body," Martha said.

"You're right," I said. "Otherwise, if he's disposed of all the evidence, we've got nothing." I was thinking too of my record at the police station. Meaning, of course, more than my word would be needed to start an investigation.

Martha cranked the van and put on the park lights and began to ease along, giving Waldo the time he needed to get out of the trailer park and ahead of us.

"I've got a pretty good idea where he's going," Martha said. "Bet he scoped the place out first day he got to town."

"The dump," Jasmine said. "Place they found those other bodies."

We got to the street and saw Waldo was headed in the direction of the dump. Martha turned on the van's headlights after the pickup was down the road a bit, then eased out in pursuit. We laid back and let him get way ahead, and when we got out of town and he took the turn off to the dump, we passed on by and turned down a farm to market road and parked as close as we could to a barbed wire fence. We got out and climbed the fence and crossed a pasture and came to a rise and went up that and poked our heads over carefully and looked down on the dump.

There was smoke rising up in spots, where sounds of burning refuse had been covered at some point, and it filled the air with stink. The dump had been like that forever. As a little boy, my father would bring me out to the dump to toss our family garbage, and even in broad daylight, I thought the place spooky, a sort of poor-boy, blue-collar hell. My dad said there were fires out here that had never been put out, not by the weight of garbage and dirt, or by winter ice or spring's rain storms. Said no matter what was done to those fires, they still burned. Methane maybe. All the stuff in the dump heating up like compost, creating some kind of combustible chemical reaction.

Within the dump, bordered off by a wide layer of scraped earth, were two great oil derricks. They were working derricks too, and the great rocking horse pumps dipped down and rose up constantly, night or day, and it always struck me that this was a foolish place for a dump full of never-dying fires to exist, next to two working oil wells. But the dump still stood and the derricks still worked oil. The city council had tried to have the old dump shut down, moved, but so far nothing had happened. They couldn't get those fires out completely for one thing. I felt time was against the dump and the wells. Eventually, the piper, or in this case, the pipeline, had to be paid. Some day the fires in the dump would get out of hand and set the oil wells on fire and the explosion that would occur would send Mud Creek and its surrounding rivers and woodlands to some place north of Pluto.

At night, the place was even more eerie. Flames licking out from under the debris like tongues, the rain seeping to its source, making it hiss white smoke like dragon breath. The two old derricks stood tall against the night and lightning wove a flickering crown of light around one of them and went away. In that instant, the electrified top of the derrick looked like Martian machinery. Inside the derricks, the still-working well pumps throbbed and kerchunked and dipped their dark, metal hammerheads then lifted them again. Down and up. Down and up. Taking with them on the drop and the rise, rain-wet shadows and flickers of garbage fire.

Waldo's truck was parked beside the road, next to a mound of garbage the height of a first-story roof. He had peeled off the tarp and put it away and was unloading his boxes from the truck, carrying them to a spot near one of the oil derricks, arranging them neatly, as if he were being graded on his work. When the boxes were all out, Waldo stood with his back to us and watched one of the derrick's pumps nod for a long time, as if the action of it amazed or offended him.

After a time, he turned suddenly and kicked at one of the boxes. The head in it popped up like a Mexican jumping bean and fell back down inside. Waldo took a deep breath, as if he were preparing to run a race, then got in his truck, turned it around, and drove away.

"He didn't even bother to bury the pieces," Jasmine said, and even in the bad light, I could see she was as white as Frosty the Snowman.

"Probably wants it to be found," Martha said. "We know where the corpse is now. We have evidence, and we saw him dispose of the body ourselves. I think we can go to the law now."

⌒

WE DROVE BACK to town and called Sam from Martha's bookstore. He answered the phone on the fifth ring. He sounded like he had a sock in his mouth.

"What?"

"Plebin, Sam. I need your help."

"You in a ditch? Call a wrecker, man. I'm bushed."

"Not exactly. It's about murder."

"Ah, shit, Plebin. You some kind of fool, or what? We been through this. Call some nuthouse doctor or something. I need sleep. Day I put in today was bad enough, but I don't need you now and some story about murder. Lack of sleep gives me domestic problems."

"This one's different. I've got two witnesses. A body out at the dump. We saw it disposed of. A woman cut up in pieces, I kid you not. Guy named Waldo did it. He used to be with the circus. Directed a dog act."

"The circus?"

"That's right."

"And he has a dog act."

"Had. He cut up a woman and took her to the dump."

"Plebin?"

"Yes."

"I go out there, and there's no dead body, I could change that, supply one, mood I'm in. Understand?"

"Just meet us at the dump."

"Who's us?"

I told him, gave him some background on Waldo, explained what Martha and Jasmine found in the LaBorde newspapers, hung up, and me and my fellow sleuths drove back to the dump.

⌒

WE WAITED OUTSIDE the dump in Martha's van until Sam showed in his blue Ford. We waved at him and started the van and led him into the dump. We drove up to the spot near the derrick and got out. None of us went over to the boxes for a look. We didn't speak. We listened to the pumps doing their work inside the derricks. Kerchunk, kerchunk, kerchunk.

Sam pulled up behind us and got out. He was wearing blue jeans and tennis shoes and his pajama top. He looked at me and Jasmine and Martha. Fact is, he looked at Martha quite a while.

"You want maybe I should send you a picture, or something?" Martha said.

Sam didn't say anything. He looked away from Martha and said to me, "All right. Where's the body?"

"It's kind of here and there," I said, and pointed. "In those boxes. Start with the little one, there. That's her head."

Sam looked in the box, and I saw him jump a little. Then he went still, bent forward and pulled the woman's head out by the hair, held it up in front of him and looked at it. He spun and tossed it to me. Reflexively, I caught it, then dropped it. By the time it hit the ground I felt like a number one horse's ass.

It wasn't a human head. It was a mannequin head with a black paint mark covering the stump of the neck, which had been neatly sawed in two.

"Here, Jasmine," Sam said. "You take a leg," and he hoisted a mannequin leg out of another box and tossed it at her. She shrieked and dodged and it landed on the ground. "And you that's gonna send me a picture. You take an arm." He pulled a mannequin arm out of another box and tossed it at Martha, who swatted it out of the air with her putter cane.

He turned and kicked another of the boxes and sent a leg and an arm sailing into a heap of brush and old paint cans.

"Goddamn it, Plebin," he said. "You've done it again." He came over and stood in front of me. "Man, you're nuts. Absolutely nuts."

"Wasn't just Plebin," Martha said. "We all thought it. The guy brought this stuff out here is a weirdo. We've been watching him."

"You have?" Sam said. "Playing detective, huh? That's sweet. That's real sweet. Plebin, come here, will you?"

I went over and stood by him. He put an arm around my shoulders and walked me off from Jasmine and Martha. He whispered to me.

"Plebin. You're not learning, man. Not a bit. Not only are you fucking up your life, you're fucking up mine. Listen here. Me and the old lady, we're not doing so good, see."

"I'm sorry to hear it. Toni has always been so great."

"Yeah, well, you see, she's jealous. You know that."

"Oh yeah. Always has been."

"There you are. She's gotten worse too. And you see, I spend a lot of time away from the home. Out of the bed. Bad hours. You getting what I'm saying here?"

"Yeah."

He pulled me closer and patted my chest with his other hand. "Good. Not only is that bad, me spending those hours away from home and out of the bed at bedtime, but hey, I'm so bushed these days, I get ready to lay a little pipe, well, I got no lead in the pencil. Like a goddamn spaghetti, that's how it is. Know what I'm saying?"

"Least when you do get it hard, you get to lay pipe," I said.

"But I'm not laying it enough. It's because I don't get rest. But Toni, you know what she thinks? She thinks it's because I'm having a little extracurricular activity. You know what I mean? Thinks I'm out banging hole like there's no tomorrow."

"Hey, I'm sorry, Sam, but..."

"So now I've got the rest problem again. I'm tired right now. I don't recover like I used to. I don't get eight hours of sack time, hey, I can't get it up. I have a bad day, which I do when I'm tired, I can't get it up. My shit comes out different, I can't get it up. I've gotten sensitive in my old age. Everything goes straight to my dick. Toni, she gets ready for me to do my duty, guess what?"

"You're too tired. You can't get it up."

"Bingo. The ole Johnson is like an empty sock. And when I can't get it up, what does Toni think?"

"You're fucking around?"

"That's right. And it's not bad enough I gotta be tired for legitimate reasons, but now I got to be tired because you and your daughter and Ma Frankenstein over there are seeing heads in boxes. Trailing some innocent bystander and trying to tie him in with murder when there's nobody been murdered. Know what I'm saying?"

"Sam, the guy looks the part. Acts it. There's been murders everywhere the circus goes…"

"Plebin, ole buddy. Hush your mouth, okay? Listen up tight. I'm going home now. I'm going back to bed. You wake me up again, I'll run over you with a truck. I don't have a truck, but I'll borrow one for the purpose. Got me?"

"Yeah."

"All right. Good night." He took his arm off my shoulders, walked back to his car and opened the door. He started to get inside, then straightened. He looked over the roof at me. "Come by and have dinner next week. Toni still makes a good chicken-fried steak. Been a while since she's seen you."

"I'll keep it in mind. Give her my love."

"Yeah. And Plebin, don't call with any more murders, all right? You got a good imagination, but as a detective, you're the worst." He looked at Jasmine. "Jasmine, you stick with your mother." He got in his car, backed around and drove away.

I went over and stood with my fellow sleuths and looked down at the mannequin head. I picked it up by the hair and looked at it. "I think I'll have this mounted," I said. "Just to remind me what a jackass I am."

BACK AT THE apartment I sat on the bed with the window open, the mannequin head on the pillow beside me. Jasmine sat in the dresser chair and Martha had one of my rickety kitchen chairs turned around backwards and she sat with her arms crossed on the back of it, sweat running out from under her wool cap, collecting in her mustache.

"I still think something funny is going on there," Jasmine said.

"Oh, shut up," I said.

"We know something funny is going on," Martha said.

"We means you two," I said. "Don't include me. I don't know anything except I've made a fool out of myself and Sam is having trouble with his sex life, or maybe what he told me was some kind of parable."

"Sex life," Jasmine said. "What did he tell you?"

"Forget," I said.

"That Sam is some sorry cop," Martha said. "He should have at least investigated Waldo. Guy who paints and cuts up mannequins isn't your everyday fella, I'd think. I bet he's painting and sawing them up because he hasn't picked a victim yet. It's his way of appeasing himself until he's chosen someone. Akin to masturbation instead of real sex."

"If we could see inside his trailer," Jasmine said, "I bet we'd find evidence of something more than mannequins. Evidence of past crimes maybe."

"I've had enough," I said. "And Jasmine, so have you. And Martha, if you're smart, so have you."

Martha got out one of her little cigarettes.

"Don't light that in here," I said.

She got out a small box of kitchen matches.

"I can't stand smoke," I said.

She pulled a match from the box and struck it on her pants leg and lit up, puffed, studied the ceiling.

"Put it out, Martha. This is my place."

She blew smoke at the ceiling. "I think Jasmine's right," she said. "If we could divert him. Get him out of the trailer so we could have a look inside, find some evidence, then maybe that small town idiot cop friend of yours would even be convinced."

"Waldo's not going to keep a human head in there," I said.

"He might," Martha said. "It's been known to happen. Or maybe something a victim owned. Guys like that keep souvenirs of their murders. That way they can fantasize, relive it all."

"We could watch his place tomorrow," Jasmine said, "then if he goes out, we could slip in and look around. We find something incriminating, something definite, there's a way to cue the police in on it, even one as stubborn and stupid as Sam."

"I'm sure Waldo locks his doors," I said.

"That's no trouble," Martha said. "I can pick the lock on Heaven's door."

"You're just a basket of fine skills," I said.

"I used to work for a repo company, years back," Martha said. "I learned to use lock jocks and keys and picks on car doors and garage doors. You name it, I can get in it, and in a matter of moments."

"Listen, you two," I said, "leave it be. We don't know this guy's done anything, and if he is a murderer, you damn sure don't need to be snooping around there, or you may end up on the victim list. Let's get on with our lives."

"Such as yours and mine is," Martha said. "What have I got to look forward to? Selling a few books? Meeting the right man? Me, a gargoyle with a golf club?"

"Martha, don't say that," Jasmine said.

"No, let's call a spade a spade here," Martha said. She snatched off her wool cap and showed us her bald head. I had seen a glimpse of it a time or two before I went to work there, when she was taking off and adjusting her cap or scratching her head, but this was the first time I'd seen it in all its sweaty, pink glory for more than a few moments. "What's gonna pull a mate in for me? My glorious head of hair. I started losing it when I was in my twenties. No man would look twice at me. Besides that, I'm ugly and have a mustache."

"A mate isn't everything," I said.

"It's something," Martha said. "And I think about it. I won't kid you. But I know it isn't possible. I've been around, seen some things, had some interesting jobs. But I haven't really made any life for myself. Not so it feels like one. And you know what? After all these years, Jasmine and you are my only real friends, and in your case, Plebin, I don't know that amounts to much."

"Thanks," I said.

"You could get a wig," Jasmine said.

"I could have these whiskers removed," Martha said. "But I'd still be a blimp with a bum leg. No. There's nothing for me in the looks department. Not unless I could change bodies with some blonde bimbo. Since that isn't going to happen, all I got is what I make out of life. Like this mystery. A real mystery, I think. And if Waldo is a murderer, do we let him go on to the next town and find a victim? Or for that matter, a victim here, before he leaves?

"We catch this guy. Prove he's responsible for murders, then we've actually done something important with our lives. There's more to my life than the bookstore. More to yours Plebin than a bad name and unemployment checks. And...well, in your case Jasmine, there is more to your life. You're beautiful, smart, and you're going places. But for all of us, wouldn't it be worthwhile to catch a killer?"

"If he is a killer," I said. "Maybe he just hates mannequins because they look better in their clothes than he does."

"Women's clothes?" Jasmine said.

"Maybe it's women's clothes he likes to wear," I said. "Thing is, we could end up making fools of ourselves, spend some time in jail, even."

"I'll chance it," Jasmine said.

"No you won't," I said. "It's over for you, Jasmine. Martha can do what she wants. But you and me, we're out of it."

Martha left.

Jasmine got out her sleeping bag and unrolled it, went to the bathroom to brush her teeth. I tried to stay awake and await my turn in there, but couldn't. Too tired. I lay down on the bed, noted vaguely that rain had stopped pounding on the apartment roof, and I fell immediately asleep.

I AWOKE LATER that night, early morning really, to the smell of more oncoming rain, and when I rolled over I could see flashes of lightning in the west.

The west. The direction of the dump. It was as if a storm was originating there, moving toward the town.

Melodrama. I loved it.

I rolled over and turned my head to the end table beside the bed, and when the lightning flashed I could see the mannequin head setting there, its face turned toward me, its strange, false eyes alight with the fire of the western lightning. The paint around the mannequin's neck appeared very damp in that light, like blood.

I threw my legs from beneath the covers and took hold of the head. The paint on its neck was wet in my hands. The humidity had caused it to run. I set the head on the floor where I wouldn't have to look at it, got up to go to the bathroom and wash my hands.

Jasmine's sleeping bag was on the floor, but Jasmine wasn't in it. I went on to the bathroom, but she wasn't in there either. I turned on the light and washed my hands and felt a little weak. There was no place else to be in the apartment. I looked to see if she had taken her stuff and gone home, but she hadn't. The door that led out to the stairway was closed, but unlocked.

No question now. She had gone out.

I had an idea where, and the thought of it gave me a chill. I got dressed and went downstairs and beat on the bookstore, pressed my face against the windows, but there was no light or movement. I went around to the rear of the building to beat on the back door, to try and wake Martha up in her living quarters, but when I got there I didn't bother. I saw that Martha's van was gone from the carport and Jasmine's car was still in place.

I went back to my apartment and found Jasmine's car keys on the dresser and thought about calling the police, then thought better of it. Their memory of my body in the trunk stunt was a long one, and they might delay. Blow off the whole thing, in fact, mark it up to another aggravation from the boy who cried wolf. If I called Sam it wouldn't be any better. Twice in one night he'd be more likely to kill me than to help me. He was more worried about his pecker than a would-be killer, and he might not do anything at all.

Then I reminded myself it was a game of "What If" and that there wasn't anything to do, nothing to fear. I told myself the worst that could happen would be that Jasmine and Martha would annoy Waldo and make fools of themselves, and then it would all be over for good.

But those thoughts didn't help much, no matter how hard I tried to be convinced. I realized then that it hadn't been just the rain and the humidity that had awakened me. I had been thinking about what Martha said. About Waldo picking a victim later on if we didn't stop him. About the mannequins being a sort of warm-up for what he really wanted to do and would do.

It wasn't just a game anymore. Though I had no real evidence for it, I believed then what Jasmine and Martha believed.

Waldo the Great was a murderer.

⌒

I DROVE JASMINE'S car out to the trailer park and pulled around where we had parked before, and sure enough, there was Martha's van. I pulled in behind it and parked.

I got out, mad as hell, went over to the van and pulled the driver's door open. There wasn't anyone inside. I turned then and looked through the bushes toward the trailer park. Lightning moved to the west and flicked and flared as if it were fireworks on a vibrating string. It lit up the trailer park, made what was obvious momentarily bright and harsh.

Waldo's truck and trailer were gone. There was nothing in its spot but tire tracks.

I tore through the bushes, fought back some blackberry vines, and made the long run over to the spot where Waldo's trailer had been.

I walked around in circles like an idiot. I tried to think, tried to figure what had happened.

I made up a possible scenario: Martha and Jasmine had come out here to spy on Waldo, and maybe Waldo, who kept weird hours, had gone out, and Jasmine and Martha had seen their chance and gone in.

Perhaps Waldo turned around and came back suddenly. Realized he'd forgotten his cigarettes, his money, something like that, and he found Jasmine and Martha snooping.

And if he was a murderer, and he found them, and they had discovered incriminating evidence…

Then what?

What would he have done with them?

It struck me then.

The dump. To dispose of the bodies.

God, the bodies.

My stomach soured and my knees shook. I raced back through the tangled growth, back to Jasmine's car. I pulled around the van and made the circle and whipped onto the road in front of the trailer park and headed for the dump at high speed. If a cop saw me, good. Let him chase me, on out to the dump.

Drops of rain had begun to fall as I turned on the road to the dump. Lightning was crisscrossing more rapidly and more heatedly than before. Thunder rumbled.

I killed the lights and eased into the dump, using the lightning flashes as my guide, and there, stretched across the dump road, blocking passage, was Waldo's trailer. The truck the trailer was fastened to was off the road and slightly turned in my direction, ready to leave the dump. I didn't see any movement. The only sounds were from the throbbing thunder and the hissing lightning. Raindrops were falling faster.

I jerked the car into park in front of the trailer and got out and ran over there, then hesitated. I looked around and spotted a hunk of wood lying in some garbage. I yanked it out and ran back to the trailer and jerked open the door. The smell of dogs was thick in the air.

Lightning flashed in the open doorway and through the thin curtains at the windows. I saw Martha lying on the floor, face down, a meat cleaver in the small of her back. I saw that the bookshelves on the wall were filled with Harlequin romances, and below them nailed onto the shelves, were strange hunks of what in the lightning flashes looked like hairy leather.

Darkness.

A beat.

Lighting flash.

I looked around, didn't see Waldo hiding in the shadows with another meat cleaver.

Darkness again.

I went over to Martha and knelt beside her, touched her shoulder. She raised her head, tried to jerk around and grab me, but was too weak. "Sonofabitch," she said.

"It's me," I said.

"Plebin," she said. "Waldo...nailed me a few times... Thinks I'm dead... He's got Jasmine. Tried to stop him... Couldn't... You got to. They're out...there."

I took hold of the cleaver and jerked it out of her back and tossed it on the floor.

"Goddamn," Martha said, and almost did a push up, but lay back down. "Could have gone all day without that... Jasmine. The nut's got her. Go on!"

Martha closed her eyes and lay still. I touched her neck. Still a pulse. But I couldn't do anything now. I had to find Jasmine. Had to hope the bastard hadn't done his work.

I went out of the trailer, around to the other side, looked out over the dump. The light wasn't good, but it was good enough that I could see them immediately. Jasmine, her back to me, upside down, nude, was tied to the inside of the nearest derrick, hung up like a goat for the slaughter. Waldo stood at an angle, facing her, holding something in his hand.

Lightning strobed, thunder rumbled. The poodles were running about, barking and leaping. Two of the dogs were fucking out next to the derrick, flopping tongues. The great black hammerhead of the oil pump rose up and went down. Fires glowed from beneath debris and reflected on the metal bars of the derrick and the well pump, and when the rain hit the fires beneath the garbage they gave up white smoke and the smoke rolled in the wind like great balls of cotton, tumbled over Jasmine and Waldo and away.

Waldo swung what he had in his hand at Jasmine. Caught her across the neck with it. Her body twitched. I let out a yell that was absorbed by a sudden peal of thunder and a slash of lightning.

I started running, yelling as I went.

Waldo slashed at Jasmine again, and then he heard me yelling. He stepped to the side and stared at me, surprised. I ran up the little rise that led to the derrick before he could get it together, and as I ducked under a bar on the derrick, he dropped what he was holding.

A long paint brush.

It fell next to a can of dark paint. Rain plopped in the paint and black balls of paint flew up in response and fell down again. One of the dogs jumped the can of paint for no reason I could determine and ran off into the rain.

Jasmine made a noise like a smothered cough. Out of the corner of my eye I could see a strip of thick, gray tape across her mouth, and where Waldo had slashed her neck with the brush was a band of paint, dissolving in the rain, running down her neck, over her cheeks and into her eyes and finally her hair, like blood in a black-and-white movie.

Waldo reached behind his back and came back with a knife. The edge of the blade caught a flash of lightning and gave a wicked wink. Waldo's face was full of expression this time, as if he had saved all his passion for this moment.

"Come on, asshole," I said. "Come on. Cut me."

He leapt forward, very fast. The knife went out and caught me across the chest as I jumped back and hit my head on a metal runner of the derrick. I felt something warm on my chest. Shit. I hadn't really wanted him to cut me. He was a fast little bastard.

I didn't invite him to do that again.

I cocked my piece of wood and let him get as close as I could allow without fear taking over, then I ducked under the metal runner and he ducked under it after me, poking straight out with the knife.

I swung at him, and the wood, rotten, possibly termite ridden, came apart close to my hand and went sailing and crumbling across the dump.

Waldo and I watched the chunk of wood until it hit the dirt by the derrick and exploded into a half dozen fragments.

Waldo turned his attention to me again, smiled, and came fast. I jumped backwards and my feet went out from under me and dogs yelped.

The lover mutts. I had backed over them while they were screwing. I looked up between my knees and saw the dogs turned butt to butt, hung up, and then I looked higher, and there was Waldo and his knife. I rolled and came up and grabbed a wet cardboard box of something and threw it. It struck Waldo in the chest and what was in the box flew out and spun along the wet ground. It was half a mannequin torso.

"You're ruining everything," Waldo said.

I glanced down and saw one of the mannequin legs Sam had pulled from a box and tossed. I grabbed the leg and cocked it on my shoulder like a baseball bat.

"Come on, asshole," I said. "Come on. Let's see if I can put one over the fence with you."

He went nuts then, dove for me. The knife jabbed out, fast and blurry.

I swatted. My swing hit his arm and his knife hand went wide and opened up and the knife flew into a pile of garbage and out of sight.

Waldo and I both looked at where it had disappeared.

We looked at one another. It was my turn to smile.

He staggered back and I followed, rotating the leg, trying to pick my shot.

He darted to his right, dipped, came up clutching one of the mannequin's arms. He held it by the wrist and smiled. He rotated it the way I had the leg.

The Events Concerning a Nude Fold-Out Found in a Harlequin Romance

We came together, leg and arm swinging. He swung at my head. I blocked with the leg and swung at his knees. He jumped the swing, kicked beautifully while airborne, hit me in the chin and knocked my head back, but I didn't go down.

Four of the poodles came out of nowhere, bouncing and barking beside us, and one of them got hold of my pants leg and started tugging. I hit at him. He yelped. Waldo hit me with the arm across the shoulder. I hit him back with the leg and kicked out and shook the poodle free.

Waldo laughed.

Another of the poodles got hold of his pants legs.

Waldo quit laughing. "Not me, you dumb ingrate!"

Waldo whacked the poodle hard with the arm. It let go, ran off a distance, whirled, took a defiant stance and barked.

I hit Waldo then. It was a good shot, clean and clear and sweet with the sound of the wind, but he got his shoulder up and blocked the blow and he only lost a bit of shirt sleeve, which popped open like a flower blossoming.

"Man, I just bought this shirt," he said.

I swung high to his head and let my body go completely around with the swing, twisting on the balls of my feet, and as I came back around, I lowered the blow and hit him in the ribs. He bellowed and tripped over something, went down and dropped his mannequin arm. Three poodles leapt on his chest and one grabbed at his ankle. Behind him, the other two were still hung up, tongues dangling happily. They were waiting for the seasons to change. The next ice age. It didn't matter. They were in no hurry.

I went after Waldo, closing for the kill. He wiped the poodles off his chest with a sweep of his arm and grabbed the mannequin arm beside him, took it by the thick end and stuck it at me as I was about to lower the boom on him. The tips of the mannequin's fingers caught me in the family jewels and a moment later a pain went through me that wasn't quite as bad as being hit by a truck. But it didn't keep me from whacking him over the head with everything I had. The mannequin leg fragmented in my hands and Waldo screamed and rolled and came up and charged me, his forehead streaked with blood, a poodle dangling from one pants leg by the teeth. The poodle stayed with him as he leaped and grabbed my legs at the knees and drove his head into my abdomen and knocked me back into a heap of smoking garbage. The smoke rose up around us and closed over us like a pod and with it came a stink that brought bile to my throat and I felt heat on my back and something sharp like glass and I yelled and rolled with Waldo and the growling poodle and out of the corner of my eye, in mid-roll, I saw another of the poodles had caught on fire in the garbage and was running about like a low-flying comet. We tumbled over some more junk, and over again. Next thing I knew Waldo had rolled away and was up and over me, had hold of six feet of two-by-four with a couple of nails hanging out of the end.

"Goodnight," Waldo said.

The board came around and the tips of the nails caught some light from the garbage fires, made them shine like animal eyes in the dark. The same light made Waldo look like the devil. Then the side of my neck exploded. The pain and shock were like things that had burrowed inside me to live. They owned me. I lay where I was, unable to move, the board hung up in my neck. Waldo tugged, but the board wouldn't come free. He put a foot on my chest and worked the board back and forth. The nails in my neck made a noise like someone trying to whistle through gapped teeth. I tried to lift a hand and grab at the board, but I was too weak. My hands fluttered at my sides as if I were petting the ground. My head wobbled back and forth with Waldo's efforts. I could see him through a blur. His teeth were clenched and spittle was foaming across his lips.

I found my eyes drifting to the top of the oil derrick, perhaps in search of a heavenly choir. Lightning flashed rose-red and sweat-stain yellow in the distance. My eyes fell back to Waldo. I watched him work. My body started trembling as if electrically charged.

Eventually Waldo worked the nails out of my neck. He stood back and took a breath. Getting that board loose was hard work. I noted in an absent kind of way that the poodle had finally let go of his ankle and had wandered off. I felt blood gushing out of my neck, maybe as much as the oil well was pumping. I thought sadly of what was going to happen to Jasmine.

My eyelids were heavy and I could hardly keep them open. A poodle came up and sniffed my face. Waldo finally got his breath. He straddled me and cocked the board and positioned his features for the strike; his face showed plenty of expression now. I wanted to kick up between his legs and hit him in the balls, but I might as well have wanted to be in Las Vegas.

"You're dog food," Waldo said, and just before he swung, my eyes started going out of focus like a movie camera on the fade, but I caught fuzzy movement behind him and there was a silver snake leaping through the air and the snake bit Waldo in the side of the head and he went away from me as if jerked aside by ropes.

My eyes focused again, slowly, and there was Martha, wobbling, holding the golf club properly, end of the swing position. She might have been posing for a photo. The striking end of the club was framed beautifully against the dark sky. I hadn't realized just how pretty her mustache was, all beaded up there in the firelight and the occasional bright throb of the storm.

Martha lowered the club and leaned on it. All of us were pretty tuckered out tonight.

Martha looked at Waldo who lay face down in the trash, not moving, his hand slowly letting loose of the two-by-four, like a dying octopus relaxing its grip on a sunken ship timber.

"Fore, motherfucker," she said, then she slid down the golf club to her knees. Blood ran out from beneath her wool cap. Things went fuzzy for me again. I closed my eyes as a red glow bloomed to my left, where Waldo's trailer was. It began to rain harder. A poodle licked my bleeding neck.

♒

WHEN I AWOKE in the hospital I felt very stiff, and I could feel that my shoulders were slightly burned. No flesh missing back there, though, just a feeling akin to mild sunburn. I weakly raised an arm to the bandage on my neck and put it down again. That nearly wore me out.

Jasmine and Martha and Sam came in shortly thereafter. Martha was on crutches and minus her wool cap. Her head was bandaged. Her mustache was clean and well groomed, as if with a toothbrush.

"How's the boy?" Sam said.

"You'd listened, could have been a lot better," I said.

"Yeah, well, the boy that cried wolf and all that," Sam said.

"Jasmine, baby," I said, "how are you?"

"I'm all right. No traumatic scars. Martha got us both out of there."

"I had to rest awhile," Martha said, "but all's well that ends well. You did nearly bleed to death."

"What about you?" I said. "You look pretty good after all that."

"Hey," Martha said, "I've got enough fat and muscle on me to take a few meat cleaver blows. He'd have done better to drive a truck over me. When he caught us sneaking around his trailer, he came up behind me and clubbed me in the head with a meat cleaver before I knew he was there, or I'd have kicked his ass into next Tuesday. After he hit me in the head he worked on me some more when I went down. He should have stuck to my head instead of pounding me in the back. That just tired me out for a while."

"Daddy, there were all kinds of horrid things in his trailer. Photographs, and…there were some pieces of women."

"Pussies," Martha said. "He'd tanned them. Had one on a belt. I figure he put it on and wore it now and then. One of those pervert types."

"What about old Waldo?" I asked.

"I made a hole-in-one on that sonofabitch," Martha said, "but looks like he'll recover. And though the trailer burned down, enough evidence survived to hang him. If we're lucky they'll give his ass the hot needle. Right, Sam?"

"That's right," Sam said.

"Whoa," I said. "How'd the trailer burn down?"

"One of the poodles caught on fire in the garbage," Jasmine said. "Poor thing. It ran back to the trailer and the door was open and it ran inside and jumped up in the bed, burned that end of the trailer up."

"Ruined a bunch of Harlequin Romances," Martha said. "Wish the little fuck had traded those in too. Might have made us a few dollars. Thing is, most of the photographs and the leather pussies survived, so we got the little shit by the balls."

I looked at Jasmine and smiled.

She smiled back, reached out and patted my shoulder. "Oh, yeah," she said, and opened her purse and took out an envelope. "This is for you. From Mama."

"Open it," I said.

Jasmine opened it and handed it to me. I took it. It was a get well card that had been sent to Connie at some time by one of her friends. She had blatantly marked out her name, and the sender's name, had written under the canned sentiment printed there, "Get well, SLOWLY."

"I'm beginning to think me and your Mom aren't going to patch things up," I said.

"Afraid not," Jasmine said.

"Good reason to move then," Martha said. "I'm getting out of this one-dog town. I'll level with you. I got a little inheritance I live off of. An uncle left it to me. Said in the will, since I was the ugliest one in the family, I'd need it."

"That's awful," Jasmine said. "Don't you believe that."

"The hell it's awful," Martha said. "I didn't have that money put back to live on, me and those damn books would be on the street. Ugly has its compensations. I've decided to start a bookstore in LaBorde, and I'm gonna open me a private investigations agency with it. Nice combo, huh? Read a little. Snoop a little. And you two, you want, can be my operatives. You fulltime, Plebin, and Jasmine, you can work part-time while you go to college. What do you think?"

"Do we get a discount on paperbacks?" I asked.

Martha considered that. "I don't think so," she said.

The Events Concerning a Nude Fold-Out
Found in a Harlequin Romance

"Air conditioning?"

"I don't think so."

"Let me consider it," I said.

Suddenly, I couldn't keep my eyes open.

Jasmine gently placed her hand on my arm. "Rest now," she said.
And I did.

The Events Concerning Two Stabbed Clowns in a Bloody Bathtub

For Karen, as most everything really is.

.

THE USED BOOKSTORE'S LOCATION WAS not outstanding, but it was unique in that it also housed a private detective agency for which I worked.

My daughter Jasmine and I shared an apartment nearby, and were thinking if I lived long enough, I might buy a house for myself and she would go on to a career in something or another that paid real money. She was going to Tyler Junior College, taking the basic courses.

The bookstore had recently been moved by its owner, Martha, from Mud Creek to a small suburb of Tyler, though other places were considered. But since me and Martha became business partners, we ended up moving where Jasmine could go to a junior college, and we would be in or near a big enough city to ply our trade, which was mostly sitting in cars with cameras and cold coffee, watching cheating husbands and wives going into places they shouldn't go. When it came to looking through people's underwear drawers and seeing stuff a person never needs to see, we were the bottom of the heap. Once we set up a camera in a woman's house to see if she was cheating on her husband. We got the setup wrong, not wide enough, and got a twenty-minute closeup of her boyfriend's hairy asshole.

We did get paid, so that's something.

Now and again, we had something more interesting, and some of those jobs Jasmine could do. I wasn't crazy about her being involved in the hot sheet gambit, even from afar with a telescopic lens, and frankly, neither was she. So, we had her do other things that sometimes came our way. Jasmine is tall and dark-haired, blue-eyed and pretty. I hate to say it, but those attributes alone can get a person through doors that Martha and myself might have trouble entering.

Martha, my partner, was bald, constantly wore a ski cap, or baseball cap, and had a thin mustache. That's just how it was. Came genetically with her rather large package. She had once worked at her family dairy, and because of it, was strong as Hercules at his peak during the twelve labors. She liked to read, so when she got older, she started a used bookstore. She always painted her nails pink and made sure that most anyone that entered her bookstore was either partially ignored or insulted.

The book prices were good. I bought books there for myself. Most of the books cost a quarter to fifty cents, and some were a dollar. Martha tended to sell by the pound, so a thick book, or a hardback, was going to cost more than a thin paperback. I liked the thin ones best, so I came out pretty good, even if no employee discount was allowed. I admit I also snuck books out to read and returned them when Martha wasn't looking.

Books and Bullets is the name of the store, as well as our agency, though I didn't carry a gun, so bullets weren't something I really needed. A book in my coat pocket now and then, but no guns.

The Events Concerning Two Stabbed
Clowns in a Bloody Bathtub

Martha had one, but she didn't go around packing. She kept a little revolver in her desk drawer next to a bottle of Pepto-Bismol and a box of thirty-two caliber shells. Our business card had a book in the top right-hand corner, and on the left, a bullet. It was hokey, but memorable.

We had a steady, boring business, and had even found a lost dog and a cat during our short tenure in our new location. The dog is home safe. The cat was found electrocuted in a tree with one paw on a highwire. I don't know exactly how it all came about, but though the kitty's name was Mr. Whiskers, from that point on I thought of him as Smokey the Cat.

Wasn't like it was a serious job, finding the cat. We took the job because it actually paid better than some of the divorce jobs. The father and mother of the little girl were rich from their accounting business. You got more than a hint of their affluence from the way they dressed, the cars they drove. They merely wanted their daughter to have her cat back and were willing to pay for it.

Here's the cracker. We were doing another job, and damn if we didn't discover the barbecued cat—no sauce—by accident.

Jasmine was sitting in a tree with a camera with a telescopic sight, taking photos of a guy named Jack Jameson who was supposed to be too injured to work and was drawing insurance money. But when he thought no one was looking, he was as able as an acrobat. She had photos to prove it.

The cat happened to be in the tree Jasmine was in, so we got a twofer. Jasmine looked up, and there was the poor feline in the tree, one paw on one of the two highwires that ran through the branches. At some point, he touched both wires at the same time and got a surprise. Jasmine said she had scoped him out first by his singed fur smell.

We didn't charge for the cat. We had yet to do any real work to find it. We said to the child that owned it that we couldn't find it. I don't know if it would have been best to have told the kid the cat took a spark to heaven, or was somewhere out in the wild, probably with a part-time job at a tuna processing plant. But that's how we chose to go about it.

Thing was, the parents knew we had found Mr. Whiskers. We showed the cat to them. We had placed it on a hand towel in a shoebox. The cat was no longer smoking—and I'm not referring to a nicotine habit—but the whiskers had been crinkled by fire and his gray lips were curled back in a kind of Elvis snarl. The kid, Sue Ellen, didn't need to see that.

Mr. Lou Cassidy, handsome as his wife was beautiful, said, "Even though that cat hated me," he showed us a small line of scratches on the back of his hand, "I had hoped for a better outcome. But such as it is, you handled it well. And we appreciate it."

Like I said, we didn't charge for the cat, but he insisted we take five hundred for finding it, and for handling the situation in a sensitive manner. Martha took the bills he offered and folded them up and put them in her fanny pack, which she wore almost as often as her mustache.

His wife, Beatrice, petite and brunette, echoed his remarks about how kind and thoughtful we were, and then we were done.

Poor kitty.

I could think of a lot of folks I'd rather have seen electrocuted before a cat, or for that matter any kind of animal or bird. I like animals, even though I occasionally have cooked pieces of certain ones and put them on my plate with a side of some sort; mashed potatoes and greens are a common choice. But over all, appetite aside, I do like animals, even uncooked ones. People I'm iffy about.

My ex-wife, Connie, for one. I'm way iffy about her. She left me for a banker and was riding high on his checking account for a few years before he decided he needed a new wife, a younger one. He remarried. In the divorce settlement Connie was surprised to find that the way things were set up, she was only going to end up with the house they had lived in, and his best wishes delivered by letter. She did get an invite to her ex's wedding, however. She declined.

Thing was, it was the cat that got us this job I'm going to tell you about. I don't mean the dead cat hired us. That would be a horror story. But because of the way we handled the missing cat mystery, the father of the little girl came to us with another sort of job. At first it seemed like a slight variation on things we commonly did.

In the end, it turned out to be a lot more interesting. I say that with a reminder about the old Chinese proverb, and curse: May you live in interesting times.

𝒢

I HAD ONLY been back from Kentucky Fried Chicken for a few minutes, when Lou Cassidy came in. I set the bucket on the table in the back while Martha fished two Diet Cokes from the small refrigerator we kept inside the office. As he walked into the store, I waved him over.

Martha put the Diet Cokes down on the table. I offered Cassidy a piece of chicken and a soft drink. He declined.

"I was thinking I had something I might want you to do," Cassidy said. I said he was handsome, but here's a bit of detail.

He was a tall, lean, dark man with gray sidewalls that made him look a bit like Mr. Fantastic from the Fantastic Four comics. He was handsome in a I Got Some Really Nice Cars in My Garage kind of way. It went along with his arm-candy wife, Beatrice, who though older than him, looked like a retired runway model that would soon have bits on sitcoms. In fact, she hadn't been a model or an actress. She, like her husband, worked at their very lucrative accounting firm. Their daughter, Sue Ellen was so cute and golden-blonde, she looked like she came from the Cute Daughter Store.

"Sit, please," I said.

He did.

Martha had already opened the bucket of chicken and was placing a chicken leg on a paper plate, slapping some gravy on a couple of biscuits she would slaughter in short time. The way she ate you could almost hear the food scream.

"This is a delicate matter," he said.

"We specialize in delicate," Martha said, gnawing at a chicken leg, greasing up her lips. "Our middle name is Fucking Delicate."

"We generally just use an initial for the middle name," I said. "You know. Plebin F. Delicate?"

Lou took that in stride.

"I figured after the cat matter, how kindly you handled that for our daughter, you might be the people I need for something more important, bigger."

"A cat is pretty important to a little girl."

"Of course. What I have for you, if you're willing, is something that wouldn't include the rest of my family. Meaning, they don't need to know about it. I need some video recovered, and I need to make sure there are no other copies, which means I not only need the video back, but need to know who's behind this business."

"And pray tell what might the blackmail be about?" Martha said, pausing in her fried chicken destruction. She had a way of seeming to want to run off clients. "Is this the usual greased weiner case?"

"I beg your pardon," Cassidy said.

"Were you filmed greasing your weiner with someone besides your wife, and now those who filmed you will return the video if you just pay a ransom?"

"Greasing my weiner?"

"Having intercourse, whatever you want to call it. Hiding the salami. Making whoopie with someone besides your wife. Parking the old Ford in someone else's garage. It all comes down to the same thing. You, Cassidy, have been fucking out of school."

"I suppose there are other private detectives I could consult."

"I suppose you're right," Martha said. "I won't lie to you. You disappoint me. I see your family, and think about how fucked up mine was, and you have everything. You both look like movie stars, have money, prestige, and so on, a kid, and you're out in the world looking for some pussy, and I don't mean your daughter's dead cat. Though I'm sure you made an effort in that department. Somehow, I thought you were better than that. My cynicism, due to your family, or what they represented, had temporarily been brushed over by a coat of rose-colored paint. It's flaking off."

"Nice speech," Cassidy said.

His ears had turned red and he had a slight tremble.

"I didn't say it was me that's playing peek-a-boo under the sheets," he said. "It's my wife."

"Same difference," Martha said. "As far as your family disappointing me."

"You see enough not to be so judgmental," he said. "I know I have an open mind about matters of sex."

"Here's why I'm judgmental. I thought you two were different. That's on me, though. I created my own happy family myth for a moment."

"I suppose you did," he said. "But there are some peculiarities to the whole thing."

"Our job," I said, "despite what Martha implies, is not to judge, unless it's something illegal. Or, let's say badly illegal. Our job is to satisfy our client. Am I right, Martha?"

She grumbled into a biscuit.

"All right," I said. "We're listening. Martha will be busy eating chicken and biscuits and will shelve her disappointment with the human condition until you finish. Right, Martha?"

"I suppose," she said, having finished off the biscuit. She picked out a fried chicken breast. I had had my eye on that. I decided to fix my plate and eat while Cassidy talked, just in case all that was soon left was the greasy bucket.

⌒

"I KNOW SHE'S having an affair. I've accepted that. She's a beautiful woman, and certainly she has opportunities. Besides our work, she attends a lot of charity events without me. She meets men that way. Or so I've suspicioned. The other day, my suspicions were confirmed. A package arrived at the office. It wasn't by mail, a courier of any kind. It just showed up on my desk."

"During the work day?" I asked.

"It was there when I came to work in the morning. Wrapped up tight with my name on it. PRIVATE FOR YOUR EYES ONLY, was written under that."

"How did it get into your office?"

"My secretary-receptionist. He said he didn't notice anything other than the package."

"Did your wife see the package?" Martha asked.

"I don't think so."

"Do you still have the packaging?" I asked.

"No. I tossed that."

"Sometimes, you can figure a lot out from the package something comes in," Martha said.

"Sorry, went out with the trash. I opened it, saw it was a VHS tape. I took it home with me that night. I didn't know what was on it, of course, but I certainly didn't expect what turned out to be there. I didn't watch it openly. It had said private, and I took that to mean it might be something our daughter didn't need to see. I also thought I'd preview it before Bea could see it. I'm not sure why I made that choice, but I think now it was the right one. The video had a banner at the first of it that said, BEST WATCH UNTIL THE VERY END. I watched. It was quite graphic, and it was Bea and a man I didn't know. They were in a bedroom. I was shocked, to say the least, and at the end of the tape were more words. It read something like: 'We'll need twenty-five thousand dollars if you want this tape back. If you want to divorce you wife, that's your business. But we will release the tape in a way that will make it available to many. How will your business be impacted by that?' Two days later there was an envelope on my desk and on it was written: INSTRUCTIONS. My wife often opens my mail, so I was lucky she didn't open the package, or the letter."

"Where is the note?" Martha asked.

"I destroyed it."

"Evidence that would have been nice to have," I said. "Do you have twenty-five thousand to buy the video? And do you still have the video?"

"I have the video. Money isn't the problem. I have no intention of divorcing my wife, unless she chooses it. I will confront her at some point, but first, I thought I should buy back the tape."

"To save your business?" Martha asked.

"To save my marriage. The business. Embarrassment for my wife, not mention myself. And then there's our daughter."

"I'd have a hard time letting that slide," I said. "My wife cheating like that. That's very open-minded of you. Course, I don't have a wife for just that reason."

"I can understand that," Cassidy said. "But I love her. I like to think this is just a foolish fling. And as I said, I have an open mind when it comes to sex, but I'm less open to clandestine activities and public embarrassment."

"What is it you want us to do?" I asked.

"First off, deliver the money. And find out who it is blackmailing me. I want to know who my wife is seeing, and show her the kind of person he really is, having this blackmail plan. And who says he won't come back again, with another copy, wanting more money? If I know his face, he might not want knowledge of who he is and what he did out there any more than I want that video spread around. A kind of reverse blackmail on my part, but instead of money, I'd be looking for his silence."

"He might not be the kind of guy you can embarrass. And it might not be the only copy. Certainly, it isn't."

"If there is more than one copy, I'll cross that bridge when I get to it."

"You want us to discourage him a little?" Martha asked. "Get your money back and a pound of flesh too?"

"No violence. Pay the money, bring back the tape or tapes. But find out who he is and where he is. I'd like to pay you a retainer. Give you a couple days in advance. You charge by the day, as I recall."

"That's right," Martha said. "I don't keep up with hours. Sometimes we're going to be right on his trail, sometimes we'll be here. But we won't be slacking either way, believe me. Where are you supposed to give him the money, get back the original tape?"

"There's a cemetery in Starrville, Texas. Thing is, I'm supposed to bring the money, but you show up with it, I'm sure he'll be glad to take it from you as much as me. Frankly, I'm worried about doing it myself. You know, case he has a grudge against me, and who knows? It could be about getting me out there so he can dispose of me. Maybe thinking if I'm gone, he can run off with my wife. I'm spit balling, but for me it's a real concern. I think you might be able to handle him better than I can, should he prove obstreperous."

I said, "When is this exchange supposed to take place?"

"Midnight. Tonight."

"How classic is that?" Martha said. "Midnight in a graveyard. Okay, let's get more details, if you have them, see about our payment and the blackmail money, and we'll start."

WHEN LOU CASSIDY left, I said, "What do you think?"

"What I usually think, and what experience has taught me. We're not getting the whole story. You thinking the same?"

"It occurred to me."

"Thing is, all we need to know is what we're asked to do and does his check not bounce. That's all our job is and all we need to do. I'm already over my disappointment in him and his wife. Can't believe that for a moment there I believed in Mom and apple pie and all that stuff."

"Cash the check we have now, and when we're done with the job, insist on the other half and cash it before we give him the video."

"I think he's good for it, but I have thought people were good for it before," Martha said. "I just got over one disappointment. We'll not give him a chance to give us another. Come to think of it, though. If it wasn't for human frailty, we'd be out of about two-thirds of our employment."

⁓

THE CEMETERY GATE wasn't locked. I got out and pulled it open. Martha drove her pickup through and we parked on the path into the graveyard. There wasn't another vehicle there, and no one was standing about that we could see. Starlight and moonlight were thin and only made the tombstones shine a little. There were some trees and some shadows at the back of the place, and that was about it.

We arrived two hours early, and I half expected they would be there too, thinking same as us, but nope. I got out of the pickup with my flashlight and a cloth sack containing some mosquito spray and a thermos of coffee. I pulled a camp stool out of the bed of the truck, walked across the cemetery to a shadowy spot at the back of it, under some trees. It was a good place to hide if no one was looking too hard for you. I folded out the camp stool and pushed it against a tree and sat down.

I sprayed myself with the mosquito spray. I hated the way it smelled and felt on my skin, and the fact that it was stinking up my clothes, but it did help against the blood-sucking squadrons.

I poured a cup of coffee into the lid from my thermos and settled in. I was there not to give the blackmailer trouble, but to make sure he didn't give Martha trouble, as she was the one that would deliver the money. Thing was, if he didn't have a gun on him, I was betting on Martha. And maybe even if he had one.

Two hours is a lot of time to kill. It's one of the worst things about private investigation, next to being caught red-handed at your work. Angry folks cheating on their spouses, they can be dangerous. Might hit you with anything at hand, possibly cut or shoot you. It sometimes turned nasty.

I thought about this and that. Remembered movies I had seen, books I had read, women I had been with, women I wished I had been with. I even remembered fond times with my ex-wife. It hadn't been all bad. I thought about Jasmine and wondered what she was doing at the moment. We hadn't mentioned this job to her, as she wasn't needed for anything. For this particular work, three of us would have been one too many. I hoped she was studying for her courses. I hoped no comets were coming from outer space to smash humanity into extinction, though I had days when that seemed like a perfectly fine idea.

After thinking about all that, I checked my glow-in-the-dark watch, and found it didn't glow all that well. But I could make out the time if I squinted. A whole fifteen minutes had gone by.

I finished sipping my cup of coffee and poured another. My eyes had adjusted pretty well by this time, and I was looking toward the truck, to see if I could see anyone coming up to it.

I couldn't.

Another thirty minutes passed by, and I studied other areas around the cemetery, thinking whoever was blackmailing would come in from some other direction than the driveway. Climb over a fence, weave through the trees, maybe.

They didn't.

I turned and saw that a mound I had been looking at as possibly a fresh dug grave, appeared to have fingers sticking up out of it. Sticks in the dirt, I presumed, but still, I had visions of a vampire clawing its way out of a grave.

Too many Hammer films.

I started making up a story in my head to fill the time, one about how a vampire was going to crawl out of the mound and come after me, and I was going to fight valiantly. I figured myself to be more like the vampire killer in Robert E. Howard's story, "Horror from the Mound." A real brawler. I saw myself as more that way than the cross-and-stake sort from the movies. If I remembered right, the hero in that story had broken the vampire's back over a table, or his knee, or some such, not driven a stake through its heart.

Most likely if a vampire started rising from that mound, I'd be out of there and in the truck faster than a hawk could fly.

The sticks did look like real fingers, though.

I thought I ought not to abandon my post, but I thought all manner of things. I took out my penlight, got up and walked over to the mound without worrying about the blackmailer. I put my penlight on the sticks. The sticks weren't sticks. They were what they looked like. Fingers. And they were attached to what was not a mound, but was instead a dead body, eyes closed, hands folded over his chest.

I was reasonably certain he wasn't a vampire.

He had on a black suit, white shirt and thin black tie. He was well-dressed and well-groomed.

Beside him was a valise.

I tapped him in the ribs with the toe of my shoe, just to make sure. He still didn't move.

"Shit," I said.

෬

BACK AT THE truck, I told Martha what I had found, and we both went over there. Martha brought some gloves from the truck, leaned down and looked the body over while I held my light.

"He's been dead a while," she said. "Why didn't you see him before?"

"Because I didn't. It was dark. My eyes finally adjusted, and then I saw what I thought was a mound, and what looked like sticks sticking out of it. I got curious, checked it out, and there he was."

"Think this is our delivery boy?"

"Be quite a coincidence if it isn't. But, as you know, I believe in coincidences. What I'm thinking is he got here earlier than us, but someone else was earlier than he was."

I said, "You think he tripped?"

"Could have, but I don't think so. No headstone for him to fall against, and I don't think he decided to beat himself to death with his valise. In fact, I don't see a wound on him, though I'm not going to go prowling inside his clothes. But I will look at this."

With gloved hands, Martha picked up the valise and opened it. "Empty," she said.

"Indicates it's even more likely he was the delivery boy," I said.

"Maybe someone accepted the delivery early. And without paying. They wanted the video instead of the money, whoever it was, because they didn't stick around to stick us up for the twenty-five thousand. I'm thinking it's someone knows the whole story. Say Lou Cassidy wanted us to bring the money as blind, to distance him, but he came early to kill the delivery boy. That kind of distances him."

"Course," I said. "We don't know a video was ever in that valise. I think Lou Cassidy would lie to a fella, but I don't think he lied about this. About a meeting being set up, and I don't think he killed this guy. Call it gut instinct."

"Whatever. I'm starting to smell some serious bullshit in all this. And it's rank. Hey, wait. There's a card inside."

Martha pulled it out of the valise. I put the light on it. It was a simple card and all that was written on it was: KARMA IS SLOW AND COLD AND OFTEN NEEDS ASSISTANCE. COMPLIMENTS OF THE RAGDOLL'S MAMA.

WE KEPT THE card. The police might well have needed it, dusted it for prints. But we couldn't help ourselves. It was too mysterious and we might gain a clue from it. Later, we could give it to the cops if we felt we had to. It had been handled by a gloved hand, so that was good. Martha placed the card in a plastic bag she kept in the truck for such occasions, so that was also good.

The Ragdoll's Mama? What the hell?

Another thing we considered was that we had found the body, and the cops don't like it when you find bodies, because first thing they think, so as to keep their work simple, is you're the last person to be with the deceased, so you're it. I had seen it before. Someone finds a body, and they become the main suspect.

In all fairness, it's because they usually are the murderer. But not always, and once the law got on a certain track, they were going to ride it to the end of the line and right off the cliff if they had to. Cops can be smart, but they can be dumb with certainty too.

To compound things, there was no tape, and we still had the money. Was the glass half full, or half empty of Fate's toxic wee-wee?

Either way, it wasn't very satisfying.

We stopped off at a phone booth outside of a convenience store in Tyler. The phone book had been stolen, but that was alright. I knew the police station number by heart. I also had a lawyer's number in my wallet. You never knew.

I called in, told the police where they could find a dead body, that I had been visiting a grave, and Bingo, there this dead person was, just lying on the ground. The location was fitting, but usually graveyard corpses were underground.

"Who is this?" the dispatcher asked.

She needed some training. "May I ask who's calling," would have been a nice question. Maybe she had wandered in during the dispatcher's break and had been asked to take over for fifteen minutes.

"A concerned citizen," I said.

"Well, sir, a concerned citizen would leave their name."

"Would they?"

"Yes."

"John Smith."

"Really?"

"Really. Look me up in the phone book."

I hung up and Martha drove us back to the office. It was late, but we wanted to discuss the events over a glass of milk and cookies.

Really. We like cookies and milk. Most private eyes keep a bottle of booze in their desk drawer. We keep a jug of milk in the refrigerator and usually an assortment of cookies. We are all fond of chocolate chip, but substitutes could be tolerated. When Jasmine baked, we were especially appreciative. That girl had a talent. She was currently going through a phase where she thought she might get a business degree and open a bakery.

Sometimes she wanted to be a lawyer. She went through career considerations rapidly, each with the same passion, and each finally dismissed as easily as she dismissed boyfriends. I hated all of them, by the way. Not the job plans. Not the cookies. The boyfriends. It's a father's job to hate them all.

WHILE MARTHA POURED milk and put out cookies, I called home, got Jasmine after several rings. She sounded sleepy. Having found a body had disturbed me, and made me worry about her. It was silly, but somehow, I wanted to hear her voice, know she was okay. I hadn't considered the time. It was close to midnight now, the time we were to have made the exchange. Of course, the Ragdoll's Mama had put the kibosh on that.

"Sorry I woke you."

"It's okay," she said. "I had to get up to answer the phone."

"Ha-ha."

"Where are you?"

"On a case."

"Oh. I could help, if you need it."

"Not at the moment," I said.

"What kind of case?"

"Nothing big. I'm sorry I woke you. Just wanted you not to worry about me."

"I wasn't."

"Fair enough."

"I'll be in late."

"You mean later. It's already late."

"Correct. Later. Love you."

"You too. But, Daddy, I love you better when I'm well rested."

"I can understand that."

Martha had the glasses of milk and a plate of cookies on the table. She placed the plastic bag with the card in it next to the plate.

"What the hell do you think this means?" Martha said.

"I have no idea. Nothing says the killer left it there. It may have already been in the valise. Nothing says the dead man is our blackmailer, though that's likely."

"They take the tape and not the money after killing the delivery boy, and put a card in his valise. To what purpose?"

We sat and nibbled and sipped milk, but no answers came flying out of our asses.

"Obvious thing," Martha said, "is we get some rest, talk to our employer tomorrow. We have to tell him we didn't get the tape."

"Do we tell him about the dead body?"

"I think so. We give him the whole nine yards. He can then go to the police, and we can back him up. Say we were working for a client so we didn't want to say anything until we talked to him."

"The cops will find that thin," I said. "I find it thin."

"It is thin. I know this. I don't like being snookered. It's almost like we were being set up for murder."

"Why us?"

"No answers from me, I'm afraid," Martha said. "Like I said before, it could be something Cassidy planned, but like you, my gut says no. It's not him."

"The milk has made me sleepy."

"Perhaps the time of night has something to do with it."

"You should be a detective, Martha."

NEXT DAY WE called Cassidy's office. His secretary/receptionist, a fellow named Traven Amrak, answered and quickly hooked us up with Cassidy.

We made plans for Cassidy to drop by the office/bookstore a little after noon, so he wouldn't have to discuss it on the phone. Asked him to bring the copy of the video that had been sent to him.

He showed up fifteen minutes after the call.

"I was nervous all night, throughout the day. I hope you have good news for me." He sat at our table, and I placed a cup of coffee in front of him, pushed some Dow Cow and sugar packs next to the cup.

Martha was stirring milk into her coffee as she spoke. She kept a close eye on Cassidy, watching for any tell that might suggest he was behind the Big Snooker. "We got the proverbial good news, bad news."

"What's that mean?"

"Means you didn't lose any money."

I placed his packaged money, which I had put in a chair next to me, on the table in front of him. He said, "So that means—"

"We don't have the tape," I said. "But it also means your blackmailer, or the blackmailer's courier, is dead. We found him at the cemetery."

"I don't understand."

"Neither do we," I said. "This guy, he was dead, and he had an empty valise with him. Almost empty."

Martha reached inside her voluminous coat pocket and took out the plastic bag with the card in it. She placed it on the table in front of Cassidy.

"Look at it," she said, "but leave it in the bag."

He pulled the bag closer, examined the card through the plastic. I thought he trembled slightly, but Martha's coffee could have caused that.

He said, "So, what's this?"

"We were hoping you knew," I said.

"No."

I wasn't sure I believed him.

"It was what was there in place of the video tapes," I said. "Obvious thing is a fellow was bringing the original video tape for the money, and he got intercepted. The killer left the card in place of the video. So, whoever killed him knew he was supposed to make the swap. Or so it would seem."

He sipped the coffee and thought for a long moment. "I didn't hire you two to bring me back this card and no video tape."

"You didn't hire us to expect a murder," Martha said.

"How could I have known?" he said.

"Let's turn that around," I said. "How could we? To let you know, we anonymously called the cops. Client privilege only goes so far. In the movies it's like being a lawyer, or a doctor. But in real life, it's like being an asshole keeping important evidence from the police."

"What if I gave you more money?"

"For what?" I said. "Hard to spend money in jail."

"How much more?" Martha said.

"A thousand more," he said. "I'm only offering this until you can find out additional information. We rule the police out if we can."

"We can't rule them out," I said.

"If you're able to clear it up without them, you can. I need to find whoever is doing this."

"Two thousand and you have a deal," Martha said.

"That's a lot," Cassidy said.

"It is indeed," she said. "But we're putting our asses on the line here. And there's this, we'll hold the card back while we make an effort to find the original video, any copies we can discover, and we'll try and find who's behind this. We don't get the video, or figure out who's who, you owe us half for our efforts. Then, I think we go to the police. I'm not going to jail because your wife was having sex with someone who set up a blackmail scheme."

"Fair enough," Cassidy said.

"No," Martha said. "The big question is, who killed the man with the valise and left this card in it with no phone number, no address. Compliments of the Ragdoll's Mama. Think. Are you certain that means nothing to you?"

"Nothing at all."

I thought there was deception in his voice, but I couldn't be sure. What does deception sound like?

"We'll take a check for a thousand now," Martha said. "We'll cash it right away, and then we're all over this like stink on fresh shit. But you have the other thousand ready to go when we give you what you want. And, as I said, we don't manage that, we keep the original thousand and you don't owe us another dime. Lastly, we asked you to bring the video. We'll have to look at it to see if it leads us to anything."

"It won't," he said.

"We'll look at it anyway," Martha said.

"It's embarrassing."

"We've seen naked asses before," Martha said. "And many of them in motion. It's kind of the core of our business."

"How do I know you'll do anything?" he said. "You could just hang onto the thousand and stay here and drink this bad coffee."

"We also have cookies and milk," I said.

"You don't know," Martha said. "You have to trust us. Or, you can walk. Find someone else. It's no skin off my vulva if you want to walk out right now. But you walk, the police know about this card and the circumstances right away, instead of later."

He thought for a moment. But not a long moment. "All right," he said.

He went out to his car and brought the video in. He handled it with care.

"You destroyed the packaging and the note, but not this. Why?"

"It didn't occur to me the packaging, or even the note could be useful, but I thought the video might. I just didn't want anyone else to see it if they didn't have to."

"We have to," Martha said.

"I still don't see why?"

"Because I said so," Martha said. "Otherwise, walk. We have some easy jobs lined up, so we don't need one like this, though I do find it fascinating. Also, we might need to give the video to the cops. Which is a major reason we would want it, so you don't destroy it and, in the end, we look like chumps and somehow the noose tightens around our necks for the dead guy visiting the cemetery with a valise with an odd calling card in it."

"Don't do that," he said. "Don't show it to the police."

"No plans to," Martha said, "but that and the card, we're keeping as insurance for now."

Cassidy wrote out a check, and we gave him back the blackmail money. We didn't mention that earlier we had looked through it and taken Polaroids of it and had sequestered the photos of the money and its serial numbers in the desk drawer in the office. Just in case we had to prove the blackmail money had existed.

LATER THAT AFTERNOON, Jasmine was with us after her classes, working the cash register as a lady bought a dozen Harlequin Romances and a Western. The Western she said was for her husband. She asked if she could leave a card with her number, so that we might call her and let her know if any Louis L'Amour books came in, as her husband especially liked those.

Jasmine took the card, chatted with her a bit, took her money and gave her some kind words before she departed. The way Jasmine handled customers was the anti-Martha method.

Martha was in her office. It had a glass front, and she had the blinds drawn. That usually meant she was mulling something over, and right now I presumed it was our new case concerning the Ragdoll's Mama.

For all I knew, she was in there plunking her pudding, but I was going to imagine mulling. I was glad she was mulling. I had already mulled and come up with nothing but more mulling.

Jasmine, who is paid for her work in the bookstore, set out to earn it, going about moving books from boxes onto the shelves. Our store traded books and bought books, and currently we had quite a supply built up, and they needed shelving.

Jasmine reminded me of her mother, without being an asshole. She was smart and pleasant. Her mother was mean and sullen. They might look a lot like one another, but in this case the apple had fallen far from the tree.

Martha opened the door to her office, and said, "Plebin. I'd like to show you something."

In her office, she locked the door. The blinds were still down. She had a television in the corner of the office, a VCR. She had a remote in her hand.

"Sit down for a moment. Watch this."

I sat in the client chair and Martha settled into her chair behind her desk. We had both turned our chairs so we could see the TV.

Martha started the TV and VCR, and up popped the blackmail video.

"Martha, we've seen this." And we had, looking for clues, I told myself. "And as much as I am thrilled by Mrs. Cassidy's ass, and I am truly thrilled, I don't want to watch this for entertainment. That doesn't seem right."

"I watch it for entertainment because of the man's ass," she said. "But what I want you to do is watch for a moment and think about what you're watching."

"Believe me. I know what I'm watching."

It went on for a few seconds. As before, no sound. Same vigorous sexual moves. Only one move was acrobatic, but personally, I like the old standards. They give me comfort.

When the tape finished, Martha said, "Now, I'm going to rewind it to a certain spot. Just watch."

Martha rewound it to where she wanted, paused it.

She picked up a magnifying glass from her desk, said, "Come over here."

I did. She placed the magnifying glass at the bottom of the window that could be seen in the video. It was next to the bed. It had drawn curtains, except at the bottom where there were a couple of inches of light.

Martha said, "Okay. It's daylight. So, we know when this fucking took place. But what is that at the bottom of the open slit? And don't say which open slit. I'm not in the mood."

"I would never think of it."

I had, of course, and was a little ashamed of myself.

The magnifying glass helped me see what was there better. It was something blue. It was shiny in the sunlight.

"I don't know what that is."

"Me either, but I have an idea how we can find out."

"How?"

"I want to show you something else."

She used the remote to find another spot on the video.

She took the magnifying glass and held it over the man's hand resting against the sheet, pushed the magnifier in close.

The view of the hand came out somewhat blurry, but I could tell what I was looking at.

"Cat scratches," I said.

"Who do we know who had cat scratches on his hand not that long ago?"

"Cassidy, when we gave him and his wife the dead cat. He had scratches."

"Look at you, all awake and everything."

"He filmed himself having sex with his wife? Then hired us to give blackmail money for videos of himself having sex with her to someone who was supposed to be the blackmailer, who was killed by a mysterious murderer who called themselves the Ragdoll's Mama? I don't know, Martha. That doesn't make sense. Maybe he didn't know they were being filmed. He was trying to get the videos back to keep from embarrassing his wife and himself. Made up a bit of a story, altered his copy of the video, masking his face out so as to fit his narrative, but still, he could have been blackmailed."

"Thought about that," Martha said. "That someone filmed them secretly, sent the video. But that seems unlikely. I think they made this tape for themselves, but if so, why is Cassidy's face masked out and not hers? Why would he say it's someone else? It seems like a preposterous lie for him to tell. He wanted to play us, why would he pay us to be played?"

"Good fucking question," I said. "So to speak."

༄

WE LEFT JASMINE in charge, and Martha and I drove over to the Cassidy house in Martha's pickup, drifted on by, looked at the windows facing the street.

95

It was a nice house, but not overly fancy, in spite of their money. In one of the flowerbeds, we could see a ceramic yard gnome. The usual thing. Little guy with a long white beard and shoes with turned up toes, old-fashioned clothes, and a blue cap. Now I knew what I had seen through the window crack in the video. The top of the gnome's cap.

The video had been filmed in the Cassidys' bedroom, which confirmed that it was likely a personal tape of their own.

"That sonofabitch," I said. "Screwing us around like that."

Martha glided away from the Cassidy house, back onto Broadway.

"What say we cruise over to Cassidy's office and jerk a knot in his dick?" Martha said.

"Can't wait."

WE DROVE OVER to Front Street and parked next to a blue jeep, went inside the accounting office. Martha gave our card to the receptionist; the Traven I had talked to over the phone. On his desk was a small placard with his name on it. He was a nice-looking young man with more teeth than a Great White, a shock of blond hair that looked as if it would go well with a surfboard and a bathing suit.

He, however, was wearing a nice blue suit with a nice blue and red tie and shiny black wingtips.

Traven looked at the card.

"Books and Bullets," he said.

"Yep," I said. "Some investigators go with a standard card. Name. Address. Phone number. But we like to keep it classy. Tell

Cassidy we're here, please, and that we would very much like to talk to him. Personal matter, but he knows us."

"Sorry," he said. "Mr. and Mrs. Cassidy aren't in today. Haven't heard from them, actually. But, they're the boss. They come and go as they want."

"This is private business between us and Mr. Cassidy," I said. "Not Mrs. Cassidy."

"Okay," Traven said. "But they keep each other in the loop on everything."

"Do they?" Martha said.

The Great White studied Martha for a long moment as if to decide what sort of specimen she was. After enough time had gone by for there to be some massive geological changes to the earth, he said, "I'll pass the card along."

I saw that he had a card in a rack on his desk. I picked it up. It had his name, the office number, and one that said home phone.

"You have your personal phone number here?"

"Cassidys insist. Why they're rich. If needed, they are available twenty-four seven, so I have to be."

"Aren't you the little workhorse," Martha said.

Traven made a whinnying sound.

Out in the parking lot, Martha said, "That was disappointing."

"Cassidy can only hide so long."

"We don't know he's hiding," she said.

"Probably went to an early lunch. Starting at about nine this morning."

"Probably," Martha said. "That receptionist. I think he liked my cap, way he was staring at it."

"Next time we see him, I bet he has one just like it."

"And a mustache? Though he doesn't look old enough to grow one."

"He'll paint one on," I said. "Mark my words."

We decided we were tired of keeping Cassidy's secrets, as he had not been honest with us about the video, and who was in it. We decided to call him on it, drove back by the Cassidy house, to see if they were home. We hadn't checked before. We had merely confirmed the gnome, and assumed they were at work.

Maybe while the daughter was at school, they were in the bedroom making another video for their own entertainment. Or for another scheme of some sort. I kept thinking about the Great White saying they keep each other in the loop. Were we the only ones out of the loop?

Martha parked at the curb, and we walked up to the house. A neighbor man wearing khaki shorts and a green T-shirt was out front. He had a pale face with a flat expression. He was eyeing us while watering his hedges with a green water hose. His hair looked like a black cap, and he had a mustache that even from a distance resembled a caterpillar.

Behind him sprinklers tossed water over the lawn. Not that there was much to a lawn that time of year, but he had that constipated look of a man who worried about his grass and ate just the right amount of bran so he could shit perfect turds. The sprays of water caused the air to smell sweet and damp. His backyard was fenced, and toward the back fence, there was the top of a single, thin tree visible.

He looked at me as if he might enjoy giving me an enema with that hose.

Martha tried the bell, but no response. I knocked on the door, and it swung open.

The neighbor had finally turned his back, was shooting the water from the hose into a flower bed that ran along the edge of the house and as far as I could see contained only short, bare branches.

Martha used an elbow to push the door wider, and we went inside. "Hello," Martha called out. She had a voice like a foghorn. Only a deaf person or a house plant could not have heard her.

It was a well-furnished place, and we stood there in the foyer like a couple of truants about to go into the principal's office.

"I don't think this is a good idea," I said.

"We don't have many good ideas."

"Noted."

"They go off, leave the door open? What's up with that?"

"Maybe they're forgetful."

"You think?" Martha said.

"No. I want to leave."

"No, you don't."

"Really, I do."

"Let's just have a little peek," she said.

We went through the living room and into an enormous den with a large television, a stereo, and some paintings of circus clowns that looked like they had been bought at a county fair while drunk. A cheap motel wouldn't have put that shit on the wall to cover a hole in the sheetrock.

The couch was large enough for an orgy that included complex positions and perhaps a monkey. There were a large number of pillows strewn over it. I mention the orgy because there were a number of tied condoms on the floor.

There were also sex toys on the floor, and a doll house in the corner. I liked to think the activity with the condoms and sex toys didn't go on while the child was present.

99

We called out to the Cassidys a few times.

Zip.

"The place seems funny," Martha said.

"You think? A carpet covered in condoms and a couch I wouldn't sit on if it was the only furniture left in the world? You think that seems funny?"

"Not ha-ha funny, but you know, that other kind of funny."

"I got that, Martha. I don't need the Cliff notes. That was a sarcastic remark."

"Oh."

We wandered about in the house a little more, came to the bedroom. The door was slightly open. I pushed it further with my foot.

There was a bed that had been slept in, but nobody was there sleeping, or having sex, and better yet, no one was there dead. There were clothes strewn on the floor, pulled from open drawers in the dresser. One of the drawers lay on the floor, broken.

"That's kind of a relief," I said.

"You mean no bodies, I presume? But what's with the clothes and the wrecked chest of drawers? I don't think that's good. Seems more like someone that was mad more than someone trying to search or rob the place. And there's still more house."

We stopped by one of the bathrooms, as I was certain there were several. The door was once again partially open, and by then I realized this open-door business was a theme.

I toed it and the door swung wider.

It was a very large bathroom with a very large tub. There was a medicine cabinet with a shattered mirror. Much of the glass had fallen into the sink beneath it. The walls were so white they jumped out at you. The white was spoiled in spots by flecks of blood. In the very large tub were the Cassidy couple. The tub was full of red tinted water. They were not bathing or having rubber duck races. Nor was the red in the water food dye. They were at opposite ends of the tub, facing one another.

They were wearing clown suits and had on clown makeup. Mrs. Cassidy had a small red hat pinned to her hair, positioned at a jaunty angle. Mr. Cassidy had a red rim of clown hair around his head. Their makeup was smeared. Their heads were above water, their bodies partially submerged, and the tips of their enormous clown shoes stuck up in the air.

The tub drain was closed off by Mr. Cassidy's ass, and the water was on low, at a dribble really, and it was just beginning to slop over the sides. That meant the murder had not taken place ages ago, but long enough for a slow run to fill the tub. They had cards pinned through the flesh on their foreheads with safety pins. The cards said, COMPLIMENTS OF THE RAGDOLL'S MAMA.

I took a washrag off the rack and used it to turn off the water.

"Now, that's some shit," Martha said.

WE THOUGHT ABOUT it. But we didn't do it.

Sneak off, I mean.

When I leaned over to check for a pulse, Mr. Cassidy was as still as stone, but Mrs. Cassidy had faint thump of life.

"Jesus Christ, Martha, she's still alive."

I found where she had been knifed through the clown suit, several strikes close together. I took a towel off a rack and pressed it against the wounds. The big ones anyway. I could see smaller ones on her shoulders. It had been a frenzied attack. On general inspection, she seemed to have been subject to a more savage assault than her husband.

Martha called the cops on the living room phone, and went outside to wait. I kept my place, pressing the towel tight and trying to talk to Bea, but if she heard me, she didn't show signs of it.

The ambulance got there before the cops and the EMTs came in and took my place. I had blood and water all over me. I went outside and sat on the porch steps with Martha and dripped.

The man in the yard was still there. He was using a weed-eater to cut some brown grass sprigs poking up next to his hedges. He was peeking at us and the ambulance.

I watched him carefully. It kept me from thinking about those two in the tub.

Almost.

The cops arrived. No siren. No lights. They parked slightly up from the ambulance, at the curb.

There were two of them. One of the cops was a tall drink of water in a too-big, blue suit. He had a friendly face, like the family dog that could hardly wait to lick you with a big wet tongue. The other was a little guy wearing a sports jacket and slacks and had the manner of someone who wished he was anywhere else and possibly drinking.

The friendly face said he was Detective Butch Long. He said I could call him Butch. He was so friendly he made me nervous. The other introduced himself as Detective Harry Johnson, which made me snicker a little. It's my immaturity. My ex-wife always said so. Of course, Martha also snickered.

Harry Johnson glared at me, causing me to lose my sense of humor, and my snicker, which had been totally involuntary, I promise.

The two cops soon had company. Three uniform cops and a woman dressed in white with a case of some sort on a strap slung over her shoulder.

One of the uniforms stayed with us while the others went inside. About twenty minutes later the two detectives and the uniforms came out. The woman in white didn't come out.

The friendly detective sat on the stoop with us. Harry Johnson did not.

After some warm-up, involving our names and addresses, who we were, and what we did, we got down to the main event.

They kept asking the same questions over and over in different ways, waiting for us to slip up. There was nothing to slip. We were telling it straight. Our story didn't waver.

"You came over to talk to them about what?" Butch said.

Martha looked at me. I looked at her. We both looked at the cops.

"Again?" Martha said. "What is this, like five times you've asked?"

"We like hearing it again," Harry Johnson said. "How about you venture out beyond coming to see them about a job you were on, and tell us the job. Give us some background here. Tell us why you're all covered in blood, buddy."

"Satanic sacrifice," Martha said. "It's a religious thing he has. He doesn't eat fish on Friday either."

"Shut up, Martha," I said.

Martha told them a big part of the story. She started with the cat, how we met the Cassidy couple, as well as their daughter. She told him what Lou Cassidy hired us to do after the cat. She also admitted I had called in about the body in the cemetery, and they should know about the call.

She told them we had peeked into the valise. There hadn't been any video, and we gave the money back to our employer, being said stabbed man in a clown suit in the bathroom tub. She told them about the card in the valise, that we had it, as well as the video Cassidy previously had in his possession. She explained that we had determined that despite what Cassidy hired us to do, it was the couple on the video. She explained how I came to be covered in blood, trying to stop Bea Cassidy from bleeding out.

Listening to her explain all that made me feel our situation was going to become more dire. It sounded nuts.

The EMTs and the woman in white with her case came out with Bea on a stretcher, a sheet up to her chin, the card removed from her forehead. Whatever they had done for her, she looked less pale, and she was no longer wearing a card pinned to her forehead.

Mr. Cassidy came out next, all wrapped in white linen, as the song says, cold as the clay.

"You know," Butch said, "a fellow could think you murdered the man in the cemetery and put that stupid card in his valise, and took the video tape or tapes and kept the Cassidy money."

"A fellow could think that," I said. "But that wouldn't make it true. We gave Cassidy back his money. There was no tape. Shit. How many times we have to tell you this?"

"Do you still have this video?" Butch asked. It was so pleasant a voice, you got the idea he wanted to pop some corn, come over and watch it with us.

"We do," Martha said. "And we already explained to you that we have it. It might be one of several, and it might be the only one. Now that we know the Cassidy couple are in on it, we lean toward thinking there is only one. And we have the card from the cemetery. Still.

As I've said more than once. But one thing I didn't tell you is that we have the goodwill of a great many book buyers. We sell cheap."

"So, you kept the video?" Harry Johnson said. "Little late-night entertainment?" He gave Martha a hard look. "I'm thinking that's the only way you're ever going to see a dick."

"I've seen them," Martha said. "Not that impressed. I have a feeling if you have one, you keep it out to pasture. A kind of penile steer."

"You freaky looking bitch," Harry said.

"Harry, shut up," Butch said.

"I mean, come on, Butch," Harry said. "This is all preposterous."

"What we think," Martha said. "But it's still true. And I'm not telling you our story again, or telling you multiple times more that we have the video and the card and we have a good selection of books. It might be lawyer time."

"I have a lawyer's number in my wallet," I said.

"This fellow you found in the cemetery," Butch asked. "How had he been killed?"

"No idea," I said. "We didn't examine him. We got our asses out of there and made the call."

"Let me give you a little information, to break the ice," Butch said. "The man in the cemetery. We know about him. Coroner looked him over. He was dead for a couple days before you found him."

"What?" I said.

"Just lying there in the open?" Martha said. "After a couple of days, he should have at least had a stink and been picked over by birds and swarmed by ants."

Butch nodded again. He was like one of those bobbing head dogs you see on car dashes or on the backseat platform.

"The body belonged to a minister named Caldwell Costner. Heart attack got him."

"I never trust ministers," Martha said, "but I can assure you, we didn't kill him, and you asked how he died and already knew the answer."

"How we find out things," Butch said. "This Costner had been embalmed and suited out to be the guest of honor at a funeral."

"Someone dug him up?" I asked.

"Nope. He never arrived at his own party. Someone got in the funeral home and stole the body. Was that you?"

"Why the hell would we do that?" I said.

"Why the hell would anybody?" Harry Johnson said.

I said, "So, the body was dumped there, and that means there never was someone killed that had come to pick up the cash?"

"Yep," Butch said. "But that doesn't let you off the hook. You still could be the ones that put the body there. Messing with a dead body, that's a crime."

"Why would we do that?" I said.

"And to what gain?" Martha said.

"Why dress these two in clown suits?" Butch said. "That's weird too. You two are at the sites of both weird events. That seems unlikely. You might be doing these things for kicks."

I was starting to like Harry Johnson best of the two. Butch was too slick. His passive-aggressive approach was wearing me out. At least Harry Johnson was openly a jackass.

"Ridiculous," Martha said.

"You're right here at the house," Butch said.

"There's other stuff going on," Martha said. "A tossed bedroom. Seems most likely due to anger than a search. There's a batch of used rubbers on the living room floor by the couch. Adult toys. You know, big, knobby rubber dicks you can stick up your ass."

"You ought to know," Harry Johnson said.

"I use the extra rough ones, dickwad. And here's a reminder. Someone needs to check at school. See about the Cassidy kid."

Butch's face collapsed slightly. "You're damn sure right about that."

He called to one of the cops leaning against a cop car at the curb, set him on a mission to have social services pick Sue Ellen up at school.

"Okay, so we break into the Martin and Sons Funeral home," Martha said, "then we—"

"Viewmont Funeral Home," Harry Johnson said.

Oh, I thought, smart lady, Martha. Now we know where the body came from. Good move. And now they might think she named the wrong funeral home because we didn't have anything to do with the body snatching. Which we didn't. Of course, they might just think she was trying to be clever, to mislead them. It could go either way.

"All right then," Martha said. "Viewmont. But you think we'd steal a corpse, dump it in the cemetery, call the law, then later we come over here, kill Cassidy, nearly kill his wife. Then to top it off, my associate here tries to stop the blood, and somewhere in there, me and him dress them in clown suits, fuck enough to leave five pounds of rubbers lying around, tied neatly. Then tossed a bunch of knobby, artificial dicks around, and waited for you to arrrive."

"You are the ones last saw all three bodies," Butch said.

"You keep saying that," Martha said.

"I do," Butch said. "I won't shit you. That makes you serious suspects."

"Two bodies, one still alive," I said.
"Barely," Butch said.

WE ENDED UP having to follow them to the cop shop for a couple hours to tell our story over and over. We got so good at it you could set music to it and turn it into a song. They let us drive to the bookstore where we all gathered up in the office. We handed in the video we had, as well as the card. I added the photos I had taken of the money, which, of course, didn't mean we couldn't have pocketed the dough.

Jasmine was still there. She wasn't allowed to listen in, had to stay up front at the check-out counter, but she didn't think the cops were in the store to argue about the fire code. She knew there was bad business going on.

Somewhere during all of that, the cops started getting calls on our phone. Solemn discussions took place. When those were finished, they asked us about the Cassidys' daughter, Sue Ellen.

"Why would we know about the daughter?" Martha said. "I'm the one told you to check on her. Isn't she at school or some such?"

"Actually, no," Harry Johnson said. "She seems to be missing. She didn't show this morning. Thought is that she's been kidnapped. Now, who was at the site of three murdered victims and a missing daughter? Let me see. Oh, yeah. There's you two clowns."

"The clowns were in the tub," Martha said. "But your math is accurate in either case, which surprises me a bit."

"Not helping," I said.

Martha grinned.

Our buddy Butch went out and closed the door. Harry Johnson asked us some of the same questions, but we didn't answer them anymore. I got out our lawyer's card with his number on it and placed it on the desk. The implication was there, but I didn't say anything about calling him. Which was best. He was cheap, but not that good.

Harry looked at the card, took a deep breath and went silent.

Butch came back and closed the door behind him, said, "Daughter says they were here earlier. She remembered the time. Too short a time to murder, dress them in clown suits and kidnap the daughter. They were at the Cassidys' office as well. Receptionist, secretary, whatever he is, remembered talking to them."

"Depends on when they were murdered," Harry Johnson said. "And, that girl is this jerkwad's daughter. What do you expect her to say?"

"Yeah, but a lady was buying books. Jasmine, that's the daughter, she had the lady's card. A Mrs. Roberts. I phoned her. She remembers these two being in the store, and the daughter too. Coroner said the clowns were most likely attacked a few hours before these two say they arrived. That's the time range the next-door neighbor said he first saw these two. Said they weren't in the house long enough to have done all that business. Had they showed up a little earlier, they might be clowned up and in the tub with them."

"Oh, that would have been nice," Harry Johnson said.

"We don't even own a clown suit," I said.

"You're still not ruled out," Harry Johnson said, pointing his finger at us like it was a pistol. "Time of death could be off a bit. It happens. Thing is, I just plain don't like you two."

"That hurts," Martha said. "We so love you."

"Best let me make the smart remarks," Harry Johnson said.

"We're waiting," Martha said.

They left with the video tape and the card from the valise, the photos I gave them, but not before Butch told us not to leave town, and ended up buying a couple of John Jakes historical novels while trying to flirt with Jasmine.

After they were gone, I felt as if I had been wrung out like a wet rag.

"Okay," Jasmine said, coming into the office. "What just happened?"

We all sat at the table in the back and Martha told Jasmine the complete story of the Cassidy couple. It didn't seem like a thing we should keep from her at this point.

"Clown suits?" Jasmine said.

"Ruined by blood," Martha said.

"And a card pinned to their foreheads from someone calling themselves the Ragdoll's Mama?"

"Yep," Martha said.

"And the child is missing?"

"Yep," I said.

"That is way funky," Jasmine said. "What now?"

"What do you mean?" I said.

"What's our next step?"

"One, you don't have a next step, young lady. Two, we don't have any steps either. We're out. Cops will figure it out."

"Oh, I wouldn't count on that," Martha said. "Who would like to think they had to depend on Harry Johnson?"

Jasmine snickered. "That's his name?"

"Yep," Martha said.

"Oh, my, I was him, I'd change my name for sure."

"He could call himself Big Johnson," Martha said. "Or Little Johnson, depending."

"Ladies, enough," I said.

"Don't dare call me a lady," Martha said.

"Thing is," I said, "we're done. That's the whole of it. We're off this case."

"You think so?" Jasmine said.

"Absolutely," I said. "It is done and done, and that's all there is to it."

⌒

OF COURSE, THAT wasn't all there was to it. Jasmine has a way of pushing, and Martha said she was pissed the cops would even think we had something to do with all this business. I think the idea of us dressing people up in clown suits bothered her the most. It could have been worse for the Cassidy couple; they could have been dressed as mimes.

Next afternoon, while Martha did some office work, I was up front, leaning on the counter, reading the paper, about how Bea Cassidy had survived an in-home invasion, was in the hospital, and it was touch and go.

Jasmine came in. I could tell she was excited. She gathered us at the table. It wasn't exactly like we were swarmed with customers, so it was no problem.

"You want to know what I found out about the Cassidy couple? Other stuff pertaining to your case?"

"It's not our case anymore," I said.

"Sure, it is," Martha said. "You always act like you're done, Plebin, but you know you want to know."

"No, I don't."

"You aren't kidding anyone, except yourself," Martha said.

"Me and Martha can go into the office and discuss it, if you prefer," Jasmine said.

They had me, and knew it. I tried to segue a bit.

"Did you know Jasmine was going to look into this?" I asked Martha.

"As well as you did," Martha said. "You should know your daughter better by now. She's a born investigator."

"I'm just going to jump in," Jasmine said. "I went in to see Butch at the police station. He was very nice."

"He flirted with you earlier, so you took advantage of it?" I said.

"Pretty much. He's cute in a goofy kind of way."

"You're a kid."

"No, I'm a grown woman and don't have to ask your permission for anything, except access to the house key. A bit of spending money now and then. Groceries. College tuition."

"Car. Insurance."

"Noted," Jasmine said.

"I don't care if you went in there swinging your naked ass with a party favor stuck in it," Martha said. "What did you find out?"

"Damn, Martha," I said.

"So, I go see Butch, and he says, how about coffee? We go around the corner, talking this and that, drink some coffee, and I bring up the case, causal like, and he says, 'I can't talk about it.'"

"That's not as helpful as I expected," Martha said.

"Yeah, but he mentions they're conducting interviews, and he let slip they plan to talk to the next-door neighbor, hear what he has to say. I mean, they talked to him superficially, but they will want to find out more. I was surprised they hadn't truly interviewed him yet. Shocked, in fact. I drank my coffee with Butch, and made some small talk, found out Butch is divorced, has a kid and a dog. Took out his wallet and showed me photos of both. The dog is adorable. I think he was getting really interested in me—and Dad, he's twenty-nine, though he looks older—but before he could ask me out for a serious date, I wormed my way out of our visit, and drove over to talk to the neighbor."

"Girl," Martha said, "you're bold as a priest who's had sex with an altar boy, killed him with a crucifix, and buried the body in consecrated ground."

"I knocked and the neighbor came outside, eyed me like I'm going to try and sell him a vacuum cleaner. He has an odd face, a little dead of expression, Groucho Marx mustache, except not painted on, and he's obviously wearing a toupee made from some kind of rodent. I told him I'm working for a private investigation agency, and that I'd like to ask some questions about what happened next door. He said 'Aren't you too young to be an investigator?' I showed him my private eye license with my age jacked up a couple years, and he let that sink in."

"You don't have a private eye license," I said.

"Oh, I do now. I made it."

"That's not legal."

"I know."

"Beside the point," Martha said. "Go on, kid."

"I told him I was working for the police, who had a lot of investigations on their hands, and needed a bit of help. If he thought that was suspicious, he didn't say so. I don't think he knows how P.I.s work. I asked him a bunch of simple questions. Like what about the two people the cops say were there when they arrived? He said you two looked suspicious, but the timing wasn't right.

"Neighbor is talky in a droning sort of way, like he's talking to hear himself talk more than anything else. He said his name was Andy and he hadn't lived there very long and was fixing the place up. He offered to take me out back to see his front-end loader. I definitely did not want to see his front-end loader. I declined artfully, and left."

"He'll tell the cops about your visit," I said.

"I know. Butch will be mad. I might get in some trouble, but I doubt it'll be serious. But here's something Andy said that was odd. He asked me, 'Were the Cassidy folks found in their clown suits?' He asked that like he expected they would be."

"Now that's a curve ball," I said.

"Yep. I pressed him by saying I didn't know, which is a little white lie, and he said, 'They wear them around the house sometimes.' He sees them through the windows, which goes to show he's nosy. Lives alone, I found out, except for him and his lawnmower, which he has named Cleveland, and his weed-eater that he calls Herbert."

"I don't care if he calls them Suck and Fuck," Martha said. "What about the clown suits?"

"Says he doesn't know exactly, but once a month, come late at night, a group wearing clown suits show up at the Cassidy house. He said there are usually ten or twelve of them. Gets kind of loud next door, music, talking, clown horns tooting, and as far as he could tell, no one leaves until the early morning. Then, the clowns come out, bedraggled, get in their cars and go home. Night before you found Lou and Bea in the tub was one of those nights when they had a gathering."

"Explains the condoms and toys," Martha said. "And their clown suits. Wait. Shouldn't they just have one car?" She chuckled at her own joke. "You know? One clown car?"

"We got it," I said.

"I didn't right off," Jasmine said. "But I do now. Oh, man. Wouldn't that be funny? If they all came out and got in one car? They missed their bet."

She and Martha had a snicker together.

"Jasmine," I said. "What did the neighbor think about all this?"

"He didn't know really, but it does add a wrinkle. He told me he thought it was an orgy, and that fits with your suspicions. He said they laugh and have fun while others weep, which was an odd thing to say."

"A clown orgy," I said. "Can't say I expected that. A regular old orgy, maybe, but clowns? Even finding them in clown suits, I'd have never expected that."

"He said those horns tooted pretty frequent around two in the morning," Jasmine said.

"He thinks they're tooting their horns while they have sex?" I said.

"It was suggested," she said. "I don't know he knows, but that's what he thinks."

"He was pulling your leg," I said.

"No. I think he would have liked to pull my leg, because he's kind of creepy. But I think he was telling the truth. He didn't strike me as the imaginative type. Naming his lawn mower Cleveland is the most imaginative thing I think he's ever done."

"Don't forget his weed-eater, Herbert," I said.

"Wonder if he named his woo-woo," Martha said.

"Woo-woo?" Jasmine said.

"Forget it, kid," Martha said. "Beeping horns, huh?"

"Yep," Jasmine said. "He said it was like a cacophony of cars warning of a collision. His exact words."

"Sounds like there might, in fact, be some colliding going on," Martha said.

"Then the Cassidys weren't put into clown suits, but were attacked while wearing them?" I said.

"Seems likely," Jasmine said.

"Did Butch reveal any leads on the child?" I asked.

"He did talk about that," she said. "Kid spent the night with an aunt and uncle on clown hump night, and they were supposed to take her to school the next morning. The aunt and uncle were killed and Sue Ellen was kidnapped."

"Butch have any ideas about that?" Martha asked.

"If he did, he didn't tell me," Jasmine said. "I get the feeling he felt the child was dead. No ransom note. Why would someone steal the child and not offer ransom? Poor little girl."

"Seems logical that the false blackmail is somehow connected to this," I said.

"We know that Cassidy didn't exactly tell you two the truth," Jasmine said, "but just because he was in the video, doesn't mean there wasn't a blackmail scheme."

"You must have taken after your mother, or a more distant ancestor," Martha said. "Maybe the one that discovered fire or the wheel. Because you're smart. Unlike your daddy."

"I know," Jasmine said.

CAT IN A tree? A sex video that belonged to the couple, or at least to Mr. Cassidy? A fake blackmail? A murder in the cemetery? A murder and attempted murder on a couple while wearing clown suits?

Clown orgies? Dead aunt and uncle? A missing child? It was too
weird to make much sense. At least in that moment, but something
was starting to move around in my head, something I hoped wasn't
an aneurism, but was an explanation.

If you're going to make a video, and you like to dress as a clown
to have sex, then why a video without the clown suits? Okay, you
don't always have to wear clown suits to have sex. Easy answer there.
I had gone my entire life without one fuck while wearing a clown
suit. Fact was, I had never worn a clown suit. Clowns creeped me
out, and to wear a clown suit while having sex, what the hell?

To each his own, but really, a clown suit?

Jesus, do they just pull their bottoms down, or have a Velcro fly
so they can... It was kind of creepy. Clown fucking and orgasmic
horn tooting?

Maybe it depended on the clown you're having sex with. I began
to think I might be persuaded with the proper clown. Smaller shoes.
No red nose. It was something to think about.

But wait, what if suddenly when you're about to reach the good
moment, a horn goes off, and instead of an orgasm, the shit flies due
to surprise.

Not a good outcome.

How many clowns could dance on the head of a pin?

I was really going down the rabbit hole on this one.

Letting all that go, I decided it might be a good idea to know
more about the body found in the cemetery, so I drove over to the
Viewmont Funeral Home, left Martha to run the bookstore. Jasmine
had a late afternoon class.

At Viewmont I walked straight in and found the head of the
funeral home, whose last name was cleverly Viewmont. I introduced
myself and we shook hands.

Velma Viewmont wasn't what I expected. She wasn't dressed in black, nor was she somber of tone. She wore a bright blue skirt that was a little high on the thighs to smack of death and flowers, graves and headstones. She wore a yellow blouse and her long, straight hair was almost the same color. Her green eyes popped like emeralds. Her smile was like a gift to the heart.

She had a desk she could sit behind, but didn't. She knew the power of those well-toned legs. She sat in her roller chair pushed out from her desk so she could cross her legs, let a high heel slip and dangle off her slightly bobbing foot.

I bet she could sell the most expensive coffin in the mortuary to a grieving widower so fast, that by the time he got home he'd have thought he bought a car.

I gave a little song and dance about being hired by the police to investigate the dead man who had been stolen from the funeral home. It had worked for Jasmine when she spoke with Andy the Neighbor.

Velma, however, was made of stronger stuff.

"The police don't hire private investigators," she said. "And they have been around to see me already."

She hadn't quit smiling, and her green eyes were still bright enough to radiate my bones, but she did quit bobbing a shoe. I guess that was her tell. When she was serious, she quit rocking the high heel. She even reached out and pushed it onto her foot.

"Okay, you caught me," I said.

"I certainly did."

I explained to her about finding the body and so on. I didn't go into all the details. Didn't say we had been out at the cemetery to deliver blackmail money. I said I had been there with my sister to visit our father and mother's graves. I don't have a sister, by the way.

"You said you were there not long before midnight?"

"Did I?"

"You did. Late for grave viewing."

"Isn't it? Only free time we had. See the graves by flashlight, or not at all."

"That, Mr. Cook, is another whopper. You get one more, and then you're out."

"Okay. I'm trying to heed my client's wishes by not telling any more than I have to, but now, I'm at the point where I have to."

We no longer had a client, of course, but that hadn't stopped us from pursuing the case. If case was the correct word. I bucked against it, but truth was, Jasmine and Martha knew I couldn't quit and leave something unsolved. They couldn't either. I hadn't quite decided if this was a good trait, or a bad one.

"I have a viewing shortly, so can you come to the point? Who's your client?"

"That I can't say. What I can say is there's a little girl missing, and all of this is connected."

"All right," she said. "Fair enough."

She had that smile again and the shoe was once again in peril of slipping off her dangling foot. I didn't even see her work it loose. I assumed I was in better graces now.

"Tell me about the stolen body," I said. "Did you know the reverend?"

"I did. Quite well. Caldwell Costner. Middle-age, nice-looking, liked to pontificate on his relationship with God. Had I been God, I've have muzzled him. He couldn't shut up. He was pretty proud of himself. Pretty serious liar when it came right down to it."

"How did he die?"

"Heart attack. And get this. Behind the pulpit. Raised his hand to God in a manner of respect, did a kind of snort, or so said his sister, and then he went, 'Oh shit,' and keeled over. Didn't wake up after that. He was brought in, and I embalmed him. Rather, I had him embalmed by my assistant. We had him all laid out in to be put in his coffin. Then someone broke in and stole the body, and you know the rest there is to know."

"Did you know the Cassidy couple?"

"I knew who they were. We had some interaction now and then. Good-looking couple. We shared some interests. Assistant knew them a little better."

"One who did the embalming?"

"Yes. You're not suggesting a connection?"

"I'm not suggesting anything. How did your assistant know them?"

"Honestly, I think he had been a go-between for them a few times so they could buy coke, and I don't mean the kind you pour on ice."

"What's your assistant's name?"

"Jeremy Cord."

"Is he here today? I'd like to see if he might know something. We're talking about a little girl's life, if in fact she is alive. Anything he knows or suspects might help."

"He's not. He hasn't shown for three days. I worry he might have fallen off the wagon. Substance abuse problem. The aforementioned coke. Normally he's up here night and day, doing something or another that is mostly just busy work, but I think that keeps him off the drugs. Or has. I shouldn't speak out of school like that about him, but him not showing has caused me to do more work than I'd like to do. I hired him for a reason. I worry about his drug problem because he's been a little odd as of late, and I think that might be the cause. Happened before, but I let him come back when he got on track. Good at his work. But he doesn't show tomorrow, I'll be looking for a new assistant."

I had to talk a bit more to get Velma to let go of Cord's information, even if she was disappointed in him, but I finally managed it.

She walked me out. As I was going through the open door, she said, "You should come see me sometime."

I turned and studied her. She looked pretty special there in the doorway, the light from a stained-glass window flowing over her.

"I'd like that."

"Nice to maybe visit, have some coffee. This isn't exactly the kind of job that has people clamoring to hang out with you. Though, I do have a few special friends. By the way. Does it bother you?"

"Does what bother me?"

"What I do?"

"No. I mean, I don't want to hang out in the embalming room, but no, it doesn't bother me."

"The buzzards take care of the dead in their way, and me in mine."

"One way to look at it. But no. I'm not bothered."

"Good. Then maybe I'll hear from you."

"Count on it."

I DROVE TO Cord's address and went up a flight of stairs to apartment 724, knocked.

Nothing.

I looked around. No one. I took out my lock picking kit. I had gotten better at it as of late, and was inside pretty quick.

There was a clown on the bed. He was spread eagle, lying across it. One of his clown shoes had fallen off and was on the floor. His white face makeup was smeared and his red lips were smeared too. His red, rubber nose lay on the bed beside him. His teeth were knocked out. He had a blue fringe of hair around his head, part of his clown get-up, of course. He was a little guy, who-ever he was, but I assumed he was Jeremy Cord. I put my hand over my nose. He had been dead awhile, ripening in his clown suit. There was a syringe with a needle on it lying on the bed next to him. Heroin, nasty as it is, didn't whip his ass and knock out his teeth.

I went outside for some fresh air.

The smell of death came out with me. Once it gets on you, it's hard to get rid of. It fastens to your brain and clothes like a leech and is reluctant to let go.

I drove to the police station and asked for Butch.

"ANOTHER ONE?" HE said. "Aren't you the lucky bastard?"

"You have no idea."

"What the hell were you doing there?"

I told him. I didn't even lie.

"You went on with this business after I told you not to," he said.

"Just following a lead. Worried about the little girl."

"Way I figure, we're on a hunt for a body, not a living kid."

"Could be, but you can't be certain of that. She might be alive."

"Right." Butch got up and walked off to set some cops on their way to the apartment complex. He came back and sat down.

"You better be telling it straight."

A man walked by. I recognized him.

"Sam?" I said.

It was my cop friend from Mud Creek.

"Oh, crap," Sam said. "What's he been arrested for?"

"Nothing yet," Butch said. "You know him?"

"From Mud Creek. We had some encounters."

"We're old friends."

"I'm not so sure," Sam said.

"Oh, come on. That little problem in Mud Creek. I turned out to be right, didn't I? Me and Jasmine and Martha."

"Yes," Sam said. He sounded like he had just withdrawn the last dollar from his life's savings.

"What gives here?" Butch said.

Sam rolled a chair up to Butch's desk, told him how I had, with Martha and my daughter, found a serial killer in Mud Creek. I thought he played it a little light, actually. I had fought the guy with mannequin parts. That's worth some points.

"Why are you here?" I asked.

"Work here. Moved from Mud Creek to take the job. Now, with you here, I'm thinking it might have been a mistake. Can you tell me what's happening with him, Butch?"

Butch told him. When he finished, Sam said, "Plebin here, he's what you might call imaginative. But he did solve that serious case in Mud Creek."

"You helped," I said. "A little."

"Thanks," he said, but he didn't sound like he meant it.

"Imaginative, huh?" Butch said.

"Wants to be a writer, I think. Kind of sees things going on where they aren't."

"Serial killer," I said. "Right all along."

"And he's not purposely an asshole," Sam said. "I want to put that on record. It just sort of runs in his blood. But he's all right. Martha, his partner, she is purposely an asshole. Jasmine, she's all right though."

"I'll say," Butch said.

"Watch it," I said.

"Meant as a compliment," Butch said.

"Listen, fellows," I said. "It's not like I've given you stuff that didn't happen, which I know was the case with us once, Sam. I was wrong on some things, but I did help catch Waldo the serial killer. Am I right?"

"You keep reminding me," Sam said. "But yeah, again you're right."

"Even a blind squirrel finds an acorn now and then," Butch said. "And that's what you are, Plebin. A fucking blind squirrel who might have stumbled over an acorn. But it could turn out to be a pebble."

"I thought cops didn't like coincidences," I said.

"True. That's why you being at all the murders bothers me. What I want you to do, Plebin, is go the hell home and stay out of police business. And don't think this is over with. Will you show Mr. Cook out, Sam?"

Out on the sidewalk, Sam said, "You made some good points back there, Plebin. You don't know how much it hurts me to say so. Butch, he knows it too. But the police like to do their own police work, so I suggest you back off. Butch is going to continue to be seriously bothered by you being at the location of all the bodies."

"You know I didn't kill or hurt anyone, Sam."

"I do, but he doesn't. Now go home. Of course, you won't stay there, and I know that. But understand if things go bad for you, I warned you. I don't live my life to bail you out."

༄

IT WAS AFTER closing time, but me and Martha and Jasmine were sitting at the back table again, having milk and cookies. I was telling about what had happened to me that day.

"You're like a corpse magnet," Martha said.

"I only have one up on you, sister," I said.

"True."

Jasmine said, "Seems there's an obvious connection between Jeremy Cord and the funeral home. Meaning more than he just worked there. Someone may have given him the drugs to get him weak so they could finish him off in the way they did."

"Or he had just given himself a dose when the killer or killers came in on him," I said. "Oh. And by the way. Sam is a cop here in Tyler now."

"No way," Jasmine said.

"Way. He just started."

"How is he?" Jasmine asked.

"Still an asshole, but I like him better than Butch and Harry Johnson."

Jasmine snickered when I said Harry Johnson.

"You're like a frat boy," I said.

"I know. Can't help myself."

"Okay," Martha said, "let's put the wheels on this thing and see if it rolls. The Cassidys are connected to a group of clowns who like to fuck in clown suits."

"Martha, please," I said, "Jasmine."

"Clowns that like to fuck in costume," she said. "Suits sounds so cheap."

I groaned.

"I've heard it before," Jasmine said, "and from you, Dad. You cuss when you don't know you're cussing."

"That's a goddamn lie," I said.

"Let's cap it off," Martha said. "What we know so far. And if you've heard any of it, don't interrupt. Plebin, I'm talking to you. I need to hear it for myself, try and put it together. Okay. The Cassidys were lying about the video being taken secretly. And it's the only copy. Certainly, Cassidy was lying about it being his wife with another man soaking his weasel. They rigged it to get us out there because they were afraid it was a setup to kill one or both of them. The Ragdoll's Mama insisted on the money to exert power over them. To scare and humiliate them. They didn't really care about the money, at least not in that moment. They knew there would be other moments. How am I doing so far?"

"I think that sounds about right," I said.

"Body in the graveyard was not only a surprise to us, but I figure to the Cassidys as well, once they learned about it. Another thing. We need to know more about the dead preacher. That might give us some clues as to why the body was taken. Then there's this mortician assistant who got the dental work and the rib realignment. Not to mention a murderous clown orgy. People killed in clown suits. Pardon me. Costumes."

"Doubt the others at the orgy were even aware anything was going to happen to the Cassidys," I said, "outside of the attackers themselves, so obviously the stabbing had to happen after everyone, except the killer or killers, left."

"You're being blackmailed, or whatever you call what was being done to them, and you have an orgy?" Jasmine said. "What's going on there?"

"I'm spit balling," I said, "but I think they were being forced by the blackmailers to do that. I think they often hosted those events, if we can believe the neighbor, but I think the blackmailer insisted they have one. Probably said bring the money again, but this time not by surrogate. I still don't think it's about the money. That was just something to make it sound like a legitimate kidnapping request. If it's thought they want the money, then there's greater hope the child is alive. What seems obvious to me, is the aunt and uncle were dead for some time, though the cops didn't tell us that. They didn't know it until they went to their house, and they didn't know the kid was kidnapped until then either. They're not obligated to tell us all the details. They held that back on purpose."

"Wouldn't the school have noticed?" Jasmine said.

"They say they're keeping her home, she has mumps, or measles or some such," I said. "They had the kid as far back as the graveyard business. At least that's the way I figure it. And it figures the lovely mortician, Velma, is somehow connected, if only marginally. Does she have some grudge against the couple? Did she have something to do with Jeremy Cord's death? She was playing up to me today, probably because she's concerned I might know something, wants to keep me close. She was reluctant to give me Jeremy Cord's address. I think she did so to keep herself from more suspicion. And someone was going to find Jeremy eventually, so why not me?"

"Maybe she just admired your manly essence," Jasmine said.

"I wanted to be flattered, but I have to say, I don't trust Velma."

"Oh, I don't know," Martha said. "Women are attracted to you until they get to know you."

"True," I said.

"The Ragdoll's Mama," Jasmine said. "I think of ragdolls as clown like."

"Yep," I said. "Another connection."

"But just because there are clown connections, doesn't mean it's actually about clowns," Martha said.

"Something just occurred to me," Jasmine said. "The paper said how Bea Cassidy was in the hospital and in a bad way."

"Yeah," I said. "We know that."

"What if whoever did this is worried what Bea might say if she survives?" Jasmine said. "Wouldn't she be in danger?"

I GOT IN touch with Sam and told him about how Bea might be in peril. He didn't hesitate, and said he'd set a man on it right away, to guard her and vet any potential unwanted visitors. He admitted they should have thought of that. I waited patiently with the phone nestled between shoulder and ear until he picked it up again.

"Done," he said.

"I have another suggestion," I said.

"You always do," Sam said. "I thought I moved away from you, but no, here you are."

"Might be an idea to look into the history of the Cassidys. Especially Bea."

"Why especially her?"

"Because she was stabbed the most. Pretty vicious compared to hubby."

"But still she survived."

"True, but the killer or killers didn't know that then, but they would know now. It's in the papers, on the news. Which is why I called you. Jasmine's idea, really."

"You think it was personal against her, and hubby just happened to be there?"

"I don't know," I said. "It could be that way. Could be both are part of whatever annoyed the killer, but Bea could have annoyed them more."

"And it could just be a nut who wanted to kill."

"Nope," I said. "Nuts, maybe, but I think it's vengeance. Careful, studied, planned vengeance. I think it is definitely personal. That's why the aunt and uncle were killed and the child was taken. And you cops know that Sue Ellen wasn't taken the night of the orgy, but before, and that the aunt and uncle had been dead for some time. Decomposition and the flies told you that."

"How'd you know that?" Sam said.

"Didn't for sure, but now I do."

"You are sneaky, but I kind of appreciate that."

"These kidnappers had a close eye on the Cassidys, and for quite some time, knew their business pretty well. Question is, if it isn't about the money, why did they take the kid, and what is this really about? What have the Cassidys done to them, or what do they perceive to have been done. I say they because it stands to reason this is more than one person."

"I'll look into the Cassidys," Sam said.

Next morning Jasmine set her sights on the Hall of Records to see what she could find on Velma the Mortician, and Martha decided to research the preacher. We let Jimmy Cord hang for the time being.

I made the bold decision to go back to the Cassidy house. It was daylight, so I was just asking for trouble, but a little girl's life might be at stake.

I parked at the curb, pulled on my gloves, and walked up to the house as bold as a man with a hard-on and a paid-for dinner date. I used my lockpicking set to get in, looked to see if the nosy neighbor could be seen, and he couldn't. I slipped under the crime tape, and went inside.

The bedroom looked pretty much the same, though the sheets were gone. I looked the place over carefully, couldn't find any way anyone could have filmed the couple secretly, which supported our theory they had made the tape themselves. Set a camera on a tripod near the bed, and went to work. Of course, the video could have been stolen. I, however, was holding to the theory that there never was a blackmail about the video. That was Cassidy's excuse to hire us to make another sort of trade that didn't happen. They owned the video and that was how they formulated their plan. He touched it up to hide his face, and came to see us.

In the living room all the sex toys and condoms were gone. I would have hated to have been the one given that job. The bathroom and tub were still smeared with blood.

I really hadn't learned a thing.

As I was going out, I checked to see if the neighbor was about. He wasn't. Probably indoors with his lawn mower or weed-eater watching yard care porn. I'm sure there was a video for that.

I drove over to the Cassidys' business office, came in and found a new receptionist. A middle-aged woman with a huge pair of glasses, but she had the nose to hold it up. Her hair looked to be not hair at all, but a cheap false hair wig with a less than pleasing orange countenance.

I went there thinking Traven might be able to give me some help, him being there when all this went down, knowing about the package being delivered. It was a long shot, and it was longer now.

"You're new, right?" I said, and showed her what I thought was my winning smile.

"No. I'm forty-five. I was new a long time ago."

"Oh, that's funny."

"Isn't it?"

"You're not a very friendly receptionist," I said.

"I'm temporary."

"Do you know what happened to the previous receptionist?"

"He quit. I was hired through a temp agency until we know if Mrs. Cassidy is going to survive."

"Terrible," I said.

"Oh, I don't know," she said. "Got me a day or two work."

The temp agency was probably named ASSHOLES ARE US.

"Is there anyone else here I could speak with?"

"I'm it. We're speaking."

"Do you have an address for Traven Amrak?"

"No."

"I see. Well, here's hoping you get three days' worth off this tragedy."

"From your lips to God's ears," she said.

⌒

I REMEMBERED I still had Traven's card in my wallet, so I stopped at a phone booth outside a 7-Eleven and checked the phone book for his name and address. It was the same number, and there was also an address listed. I memorized it. I decided not to call, but would instead drive to his place.

Back in the car I pulled a map from the glovebox and gave it a check. It wasn't far from where I was. I found the duplex with his number on it. Upstairs, number two.

I knocked. My knock echoed.

I walked to the window. The curtains were parted. Except for a couch and a couple of lonely wooden chairs that looked as if they were too shy to fuck, but wanted to, there was nothing.

I went downstairs thinking about how those chairs would have sex. Lots of sawdust, I figured.

Defeated, I drove back to the bookstore.

⌒

ME AND MARTHA were sitting at the store table drinking coffee when Jasmine came in. Martha was holding out the information she had acquired until the kid could arrive.

Jasmine came in swirling a flowery dress, looking as fresh as a spring morning. I could tell she was excited.

When Jasmine sat down, Martha said, "From what I could find
out, the preacher wasn't any worse than any other grifter that ever
passed an offering plate."

"That's mean, Martha," Jasmine said.

"Meant to be," Martha said. "I don't like preachers. I don't like
churches that don't pay taxes. I don't like evangelists. I don't like
crackers and grape juice in place of bread and wine. And come to
think of it, I don't like bread and wine. I have a limited view of religion, I admit. Some of the music is good if you forget the words."

"That's all you found out?" I said. "That you don't like religion."

"Well, he died at the pulpit," she said.

"That part I told you about," I said.

"I know," she said. "Just saying I know that. But here's something you don't know. I found one of his relatives and went to
visit her. Barbara is her name. She didn't care for him, but was
the one that claimed the body and was arranging the funeral until
Velma took it over from her. Velma offered that assistance right
away. Barbara was alright with that. She said he was a Sad Sack
kind of guy and often threatened suicide, and disappointed his
family members by not doing it. Barbara knew he had been married twice, and spent some time in prison for a Ponzi scheme, but
she didn't know his wives or much about anything that had to do
with him."

"But why was his body stolen?" I asked.

"That is all she knew."

Jasmine had been vibrating while Martha talked, and only her
good manners kept her from leaping in earlier.

"Velma was the preacher's former wife," Jasmine said. "Velma
didn't mention that to you, did she?"

"No," I said.

"She not only arranged the funeral, but paid for it with her own money."

"And where did you learn this?" I said.

"Butch. He likes me, you know. Get to talking to him, he's plain blabby. Said he saw you and Sam this morning, right before he came to our lunch date."

"He didn't mention a lunch date," I said. "Neither did you."

"You know," Jasmine said, "Butch is actually kind of cute, and would be cuter if he had a suit that fit. He could jump around inside those he wears."

"Cute?" I said.

"A little old for me, but not in a creepy way. He said Velma they looked at, and the only thing they found was the preacher dude had been married to her some years ago, and they were still friendly."

"They are suddenly very happy with coincidence," I said. "I find bodies, I make them nervous, they find all manner of connections and they dismiss them."

"I don't think that," Jasmine said. "I think they just couldn't connect it to the Cassidy case in a way that mattered. I'm sure they're still looking to link everything up."

"Before we had a lot of shit that didn't add up," Martha said. "Now we have more shit that doesn't add up."

"Yep," I said, "but we know the components of the shit, just don't know the proper mixture."

We sat at the table in silence for a while, trying to find the solution.

"I got nothing," Jasmine said.

"Me either," Martha said.

"Another thing I'm curious about," I said. "The receptionist at the accounting firm. He's suddenly gone."

"I don't know there's anything in that," Martha said. "He sees his employment status fading and he's jumped ship to find something else. Makes sense. Good-looking young man."

"Oh," Jasmine said.

"Forget it," I said.

I guess we bounced ideas around for another hour or so. Enough Martha brought out the milk and cookies. We sipped milk and ate cookies and cast our theories all about like chum on the water. No solution-sharks bit.

Our phone rang.

"I think you ought to get up and answer that," Martha said. "I'm deep into the cookie zone."

We have two lines. One in the office, the other at the counter. I answered it at the counter.

It was Sam.

Ꮘ

"I SHOULDN'T BE sharing this," Sam said, "but since Butch is kind of dating your daughter—"

"Dating?"

"Kind of. And we're friends, and I feel sorry for you if she is. But as a way of softening the dating blow, I thought I'd toss you some information, as you're onto more concerning this case than we are. That surprises me. You always seem so wrong about everything. Now, brace yourself. Get this. The mortician and the preacher were once married."

"You're behind the eight ball on that one," I said.

"You knew?"

"Yep." I didn't mention that Butch blabbed, though I wanted to.

"All right. Here's something else," Sam said. "The bacon for the pan. The Cassidys have a checkered history. They were hot shot lawyers back in the day, and their names were different. Same first names. But their last name was Abbot then. One night about ten years ago in a Dallas suburb, Bea Cassidy, then Bea Abbot, had a little too much to drink at a Halloween party. Hubby drank even more, so she was the one decided to drive them home. She was the lesser drunk designated driver. She shouldn't have been in charge of a wheelbarrow, let alone a car, alcohol level she turned out to have.

"She's driving, hubby is sleeping in the passenger seat, and down the street there's a bunch of trick-or-treaters. Six of them, to be exact. And they're costumed, as were the Abbots, by the way, and the kids are walking right toward the car, near a construction site. There's this big pile of gravel and concrete slabs there, dumped by a truck earlier that day. Filler for something or another.

"Bea swerved, went into the pile, and it shifted. It fell over the car and spread out into the street. The kids scattered. Five of them. The sixth, a girl of about nine, she didn't scatter. The gravel and such tumbled over her.

"Neighbors came out and saw what had happened. Called the cops, emergency crew, the street department, fire department. The whole batch.

"Turns out it was easy to get the Abbots out of the car. Cops said Bea was wearing some kind of genie outfit that showed a lot of flesh. That was in the records, what she was wearing. Male cops, of course. No mention what hubby was wearing, other than a costume.

"But here's the thing. The little girl was alive in that pile. Concrete slabs had shifted in such a way that it made a kind of shelter from the gravel and the rest of the slabs. There was hope. The rescue party could talk to her. She could talk back. Thing was, the slab was shifting, gravel was slipping in from the sides, slowly. It was such a precarious pile, and by the time equipment that was needed got there, things had gone really bad. Stuff had shifted again. They worked for days to get the little girl out. She talked to them. They were so close. Eventually she quit talking. They could hear the gravel shifting, and then they could hear the slab shifting too. They got her out, but it was too late. She was dressed as a ragdoll for Halloween. That ring a bell?"

"It does."

"Doctor said she wasn't crushed. Gravel and slab had shifted, but it didn't crush her, way the slab was hung up on other stuff, but she was pinned in this small space with little air. She used it up. She suffocated. The mother of the little girl, Judy Paul, was just down the street with her husband, Jim Paul. It was the family's street. Their house was nearby. The mother was there when they pulled her child, Ripley, out in her bloody costume. Later, when she found out the way the kid died was by asphyxiation, she lost it. The idea of that slow death was too much for her. Committed suicide three weeks after. Drove out to a stretch of Highway 80, waited out on the high-way by her car and ran out in front of a semi that was really balling the jack. Nothing the driver could do. She was killed instantly and sprinkled about like wet meat rain."

"Damn," I said.

"That wasn't bad enough on the Paul family, the father took to drink, got in a bar fight over hardly anything at all, and was smacked in the kisser with a bottle. Glass made a mess of his face. They had to redo his teeth, and his required facial surgery."

"When it rains it pours," I said.

"Lot of people made a lot of bad decisions. The Abbots were brought to trial, and it took a while for the law to get them there, as they had good lawyers. Once there, Bea was able to get off with a DUI. Way the lawyers played it, it was the kids' fault, being in the street, and Bea had to swerve, and by doing so she saved five lives and only one was lost. They made it look like a win."

"Fucking lawyers."

"The father was devasted. Saw some old video of him on the steps of the courthouse being asked about the conclusion of the trial. What he thought. You know, usual dumb ass reporter question when it's obvious what he thought. He's standing there with his face in bandages from a bout of surgery, standing there like a fucking mummy, and this reporter is asking him this shit. Mr. Paul said all he could think about was his child slowly smothering under all that debris. About his wife in so much pain she was willing to run out in front of a truck. Said he hoped if the couple ever had a child that it smothered to death like his baby, the little ragdoll. Thing is, though, the ragdoll's mother is dead, and years ago."

"Do you have photos or newspaper clippings from that time, or do I need to research that, which I'd rather not have to do? Need I mention Waldo the Great again?"

"You need not. We have copies of all that here. I have a video of the interview with the father. Made a copy. I'll drop them by your store in short time."

"Appreciated. Anything else?"

"Besides the daughter, Ripley, there was a son, Vernon, thirteen years old. That's really all that's known about the Pauls. After the trial they packed up and went away. Can't be located in any kind of records since. Journalists have looked, hoping to have a good story. But when the father and son went off track, they did it well. The father had a construction business, a fairly successful one, sold it out for serious money, so he's financed. Might be doing construction somewhere else, something related. But he and Vernon disappeared good. May have changed his name like the Abbots, but not legally. Probably put together a new identity for himself and his son."

"But why?" I asked.

"To distance them from what happened. I can't say other than that. Remember, you didn't hear this from me. You can do things and go places we cops can't. Can't tell you to do anything, and if you break the law, get caught, it could cause you some serious trouble. Not like I'm giving you permission."

"I understand."

When I went back to the table, I told Jasmine and Martha what I had been told by Sam.

"A child for a child," Martha said.

"Seems like," I said.

"Then we have to go in full force," Jasmine said.

"Martha," I said. "You and me need to go to the funeral home tonight, see if we can find some connection to the little girl, or the Cassidys. Jasmine, maybe you can find out how Bea is doing, if she can talk?"

"I'll have to skip a class."

"Skip it," I said.

ME AND MARTHA and her golf club waited until midnight and went over to the funeral home. She leaned the club against the wall and picked the lock on the back door. She recovered the club, we went in.

We were on a stage with a pulled curtain in front of us. The stage was where caskets with bodies were displayed. Stage had steps leading down to an auditorium.

We could hear voices. A low mumble tide punctuated by laughs and even a clown horn that honked now and then. Light leaked in at the corners between curtain and walls.

While Martha leaned on her golf club, I tiptoed over to the edge of the curtain and gently moved it a short space and looked out. The room was full of clowns. Circus clowns, rodeo clowns. They were gathered around a long table stacked with snacks.

I let go of the edge of the curtain and tiptoed back to Martha. "The place is full of clowns. They're drinking and eating cheese and crackers."

"Yeah, I figured the honking wasn't geese."

We slipped off the stage and took a walk through an open door and into deeper darkness, which we illuminated slightly with our penlights.

It was a room full of coffins.

"These would make great storage chests," Martha said, moving her light over the caskets.

A slight sound of movement. The creak of a door being opened. Just as I swung my penlight toward the door there was a blaring sound that nearly made me shit a turd the size of the Taj Mahal with an adjacent storage unit.

The sound was a clown horn.

The light was turned on. The room began to fill with clowns; they flowed through an open doorway.

One of the clowns, a big fat one, held a big fat gun with a long barrel. It was pointed at us.

"Now we got you," the clown said, and pulled the trigger.

CLOTH FLOWERS EXPLODED from the end of the gun and the clown made with a giggle that caused the hair on the back of my neck to stand up.

Martha yelled "Fore," swung her golf club and nailed the clown upside the head. He dropped like an anvil and soiled his clown pants. I could smell it.

Martha said, "Fucking hole in one."

"Stop, it was a joke," said one of the clowns. It was a female clown with a big red nose and a white-powder painted face and a blue mini-skirt so short it almost ended under her navel. The dress had an enormous rainbow-colored bow fastened at the waist. She wore ripped, black, fishnet stockings and big floppy clown shoes. Her hair was a blue fright wig.

I recognized that smooth as velvet voice, those liquid eyes.

Velma.

The clowns were closing in on us. Martha rested the club on her shoulder said, "Which one of you motherfuckers is next?"

No motherfuckers volunteered. They quit moving forward.

"I just want you to know I hate you guys," Martha said.

"You don't know us," Velma said.

"I know I hate clowns," Martha said. "And I know you have your fingers in some rotten pies, woman, and that puts you on my doo-doo list."

"Let's rough 'em up," said one of the male clowns. "The bitch knocked the shit out of Larry."

"Come try that," Martha said. "See if I can make a hole in one with you."

"No," Velma said. "Would everyone please go back to your enjoyment. I'll join you later. Without my underpants."

A horn in the back honked, someone said, "Hot damn."

The clowns helped the one on the floor up. "He seems all right," one of the clowns said, "but he's got a knot the size of an orange."

Velma said, "Someone wipe his ass and take him to the showers in the back. Close the door on the way out."

Another honk, and the clown was lifted up and hauled away. The door was closed. Another honk outside the door.

"I'm thinking about pressing charges," Velma said.

"Connections we got with you on Lou Cassidy's death, Bea in the hospital. Doesn't look good for you. So call them."

"I had nothing to do with that. I can't speak for everyone here at the party, but I have done nothing wrong, outside of breaking social barriers."

"You mean clown orgies?" Martha said.

"Tonight, you have broken the spell. It'll most likely be crackers and wine for me, nothing else. I'm a little dry now."

"Thirsty?" I asked. "Oh. The other?"

"Both. Listen, let's go in here, in the lounge where we can talk. I really think you need to hear what I have to say, just so you know where we're coming from. Where I'm coming from. If for no other reason than you'll leave us alone. I hope."

I thought, fine, talk away. I was going to be looking for holes in her conversation.

In the lounge we sat in some nice comfy chairs. Velma looked at me. "Does me dressed like this make you nervous?"

She sat with her legs crossed and the clown shoe dangling. It was a thing with her.

"Just curious," I said.

"There are a lot of us who love clowns, the idea of clowns, so, gradually the group was put together and grew. The notion of sex in our clown makeup and garb arrived slowly. We don't find it weird at all."

"Did those feelings arrive by clown car?" Martha said.

"Good. A joke. We like jokes. But you can't assume we are murderers because those in our group share an uncommon interest. Each have our reasons for our attraction to clowns. When I was a child there was a children's TV show that had a clown as its host. A lady clown. She was always wearing cute clown makeup and telling jokes a kid could laugh at. I liked it. It was different than my home where nothing was funny and my parents hated one another. Either my mother or my father sported a black eye weekly. Sometimes it was both. My mother hated my father because he was a narcissist, my father hated my mother because she had gotten old. Understand, she was only forty, and quite beautiful, and he was in the same age ballpark, losing his hair and gaining a belly. He gave her holy hell for gaining a few pounds and having a gray hair or two. But their problems were much deeper than that. And this clown, I watched her children's show into adulthood, and one day, I realized I couldn't tell she had aged. The makeup."

"You escaped into TV show clown land because your life was so sad and Daddy thought Mommy wasn't as pretty as he wanted her to be?" Martha said. "Mark me up for not giving a shit. Look at me. Look at you. You won the genetic lottery. I got a tin cup and no pencils to sell, so pardon me if I'm not crying a river."

"I don't expect you to understand, but I'm trying to explain who we are, or who I am, and get your nose out of my business. I am harmless. I'm not a killer."

"But you didn't mention your ex-husband was the stolen corpse," I said.

"Why should I? You're not the police."

She had me there.

"You think I'm guilty—that our group is guilty—because we have this particular interest. You'd call it a fetish. We call it a lifestyle. I call it a place to go. You see me on a normal day, I'm just this hot-looking woman with a peculiar job. And you'd be surprised how my appearance mixed with my profession turn some men and women on."

"Please, don't be so goddamn modest," Martha said.

"Why be falsely modest? I'm trying to explain something here."

"Will we be needing a blanket and a snack?" Martha said. "You got us. We snuck in. Call the cops, or get your sob story told. But don't think you're off the hook, either way."

"Thing about clown makeup, even as you age, even as that hotness I have grows cool, when I'm a clown, I'm always the same. Bones shift. Jaws sag. Wrinkles show up, but that won't matter."

"Yeah," Martha said. "But you'll still be a fucking clown."

"A noble art," Velma said, and then looked at me. "I really did invite you to go out with me because I found you attractive, Plebin. It wasn't anything else. I believe now you thought I was trying to pump you for information. I couldn't see how going for coffee could hurt either one of us."

"He has coffee at the bookstore," Martha said.

"Well, it's nothing now," Velma said. "Coffee or otherwise."

"I can live with that," I said. "Tell us this. Were you at that get-together where the Cassidys were stabbed?"

"I was. So was everyone here. And there were others. There is another clown group that comes from out of town to meet up with us from time to time. There are occasionally stray clowns. But they come with an invite from members. We're like a club."

"So, could you tell if someone you didn't know was at a gathering?" Martha asked.

"It's not that secret. We recognize the way people do makeup, dress. Of course."

"Was there anyone at the Cassidy house orgy night that you didn't know?"

"The clowns from Lufkin we didn't know, and there were a couple of clowns that didn't actually take part in the gathering, but had been invited."

"By the gathering, you mean the sex?" I asked.

"Exactly. They were just there. Very polite, but if they were approached, they deferred, and they didn't approach anyone."

"Who invited them?" Martha asked.

"I don't know. I assumed they had been invited. I can't be certain. Didn't seem deep in the lifestyle, clowns or sex. Sloppy makeup. I think they may have been there merely to watch the sex. Voyeurs. Can't say for sure. Now that I think about it, it did seem they were focused on the Cassidys. Lot of us were. Beautiful couple. It was nice to interact with them."

"As in bolt and washer?" Martha said.

"You could say that."

I said, "Your assistant, dead now, as I'm sure you know—"

"Of course."

"—was he there?"

"Yes. One reason I hired him, is he's in…was in, the lifestyle."

"Besides a bunch of grown-ups in clown suits, nothing seemed odd that night?" Martha said.

"Nothing I noted," Velma said. "But I was quite busy."

"Aren't you the little revolving door," Martha said.

VELMA DIDN'T CALL the cops. She just asked us to leave, and we did.

As we climbed into the car, I said, "So what did we learn there?"

"That Velma is one weird pussy cat."

"She has an interest in something we don't share, but it doesn't make her a killer, and she's only odd because we don't share her interests."

"Look, dressing up like a clown and fucking each other, having a little wine and cheese on the side, I got nothing against. I wish I could get some fucking. But that whole bit of business paints over something darker in my view. Remember, John Wayne Gacy was a fucking clown. Remember, he said 'clowns can get away with murder'."

"Ronald McDonald is a clown, but he's not out murdering people, unless you count clogged arteries."

"So you say."

"The Pauls, they're the two strange clowns," I said. "Has to be."

"Seems so."

"And Traven knows something."

"And of course, Traven is Jim Paul's son."

⌒

NEXT MORNING, BACK at the bookstore, we sold a few books, and did nothing else about the case because we didn't know anything else to do.

Oh, we looked through the clippings and such Sam had sent over. It was pretty much old news now. But I did study the photos of Mr. Paul and his son, a photo of the now dead wife. It depressed me. Especially one of the later ones where Mr. Paul's face was bandaged up from the beating he took.

We made some lunch by microwaving burritos and opening up some sodas. We were eating when the phone rang.

It was Jasmine.

"Dad, Mrs. Cassidy is coming around. You and Martha ought to get up here. I been waiting in the hallway, and Butch came up to feed me in the hospital cafeteria—not recommended, by the way, though I hear the corndogs are to die for—but he told me Mrs. Cassidy had survived and is able to talk a little. Sam is here too. He said he thought he could make it work, us speaking to her."

"On the way."

⌒

HOSPITALS HAVE ALWAYS depressed me and the smell of them is part of it. Disinfectant perhaps. Waste matter, the specter of death, you name it. Hospitals are about healing, but that isn't what I think of when I walk into those bright and sterile buildings. I've lost loved ones in hospitals, friends too. We went down a hall, rode an elevator to the second floor, down another hall where two cops sat in chairs outside a room.

One of the cops was in uniform. The other was not. It was Sam. He stood up when he saw us.

He said, "I can give you five, maybe ten minutes, and I got to say, if asked, I let you go in because I thought she might talk to you easier than us, seeing how her husband was a client. Don't know there's anything to that, but that's the story. I let Jasmine slip in earlier. She did that to fill Mrs. Cassidy in on how you were involved with her husband beyond the search for the cat. I'm sure she knew, but I took it like she didn't. Me, I'm going home for a while."

I thanked him and we went inside. The room was practically covered in flowers. It was like walking through a jungle. There was all manner of arrangements. Even one arrangement with four black roses. They appeared to be made of plastic.

Bea was propped up, as the bed was raised. Her hair was spread out over the pillow like a blonde explosion. He eyes looked wild, like a cow realizing the line she was in was not a food line but was for the butcher's hammer. She had tears in her eyes and on her cheeks. Even wearing that mask of pain and sorrow, she was quite beautiful.

Jasmine sat in a chair beside the bed. She was holding Bea's hand.

Good touch. That might make Bea feel more secure. Talkative. Which is not to say the gesture was less than natural kindness on Jasmine's part.

Me and Martha stood by the bed.

"Bea," I said, "I know the cops have asked, and you've only been awake for a short time, but is there something you might tell us you haven't told them? We know about the gatherings. We know your daughter was missing before the gathering."

"I told them all I know. We had a…gathering. And then early morning, when everyone started home, and we locked up, we realized two of the group had stayed behind. Out of sight. They had been there to watch, and that was it. We only allow that one time at our house, when we host, and then they will no longer be invited. They have to participate."

"You invited them?" Martha asked.

"No. Others in the group can invite, so we assumed that was the case, but I can't say for sure. I didn't recognize them or their makeup. It wasn't well done."

Velma had said pretty much the same.

"You see, the kidnappers left a note for Lou, said we had to host a gathering, even though we didn't want to, not with Sue Ellen missing. But we were following orders out of fear of what might happen to our baby. We had to go through with everything. Even the sex. By this point, I assumed it was one of the two we didn't know that were involved, or both. That they were the kidnappers. We expected either we were being played for fun, or they would ask for money again when everyone left. Make arrangements with us to return Sue Ellen. We had to chance it. It was so cruel. All of it.

"When the others were gone, one of the ones we didn't know, the older one, though I couldn't tell you how much older, just older, he suddenly had a gun. He pointed it at us. He had us go to the bathroom, and then made us sit in the tub. Then the younger one, he pulled a knife, sprang on us and started stabbing. He was laughing while he did it. I think it surprised the older one a little. Maybe that wasn't the plan."

"Not even a hint of who they may have been?"

"Well, I remember thinking the younger clown, who wore some really heavy makeup, and didn't speak, only laughed, was really familiar. I was so frightened. So surprised. My mind wasn't working right. But I'm pretty sure him I know. Now my sister and my brother-in-law are dead, and my lovely daughter is missing. Kidnapped. I'm confused. I'm scared for my baby…I've lost everything."

Her brows wrinkled; her head turned to the side. "The man, when he pointed the gun and spoke, I was certain I had heard that voice before. Like the younger one, who didn't speak, there was something familiar about both of them."

"But no one comes to mind?" Martha asked.

"Not really."

"What did the older one say?" Martha said.

"Mainly just orders. But once we were forced into the tub, I think he had a lecture planned, but the younger one, he kind of lost it. Started stabbing us. All I remember was Lou's back must have slid over the faucet knob, turned on the water. I could hear the water dripping. Later, I could feel it rising. It made me sleepy. I was so weak. I could actually feel my life oozing out. And then I understand from Jasmine you two found us, saved me. Thank you for that."

"That's all right," I said. "We should let you rest."

"You will find my daughter? You will look? I'll pay. I'll pay what you want."

"We're looking," Martha said. "You can count on that."

Out in the hall we nodded at the cop. Sam was already gone. We started walking toward the elevator. When we were inside and heading down, Jasmine pulled out a small card, said, "I had to wait to mention it. It was on one of the flower arrangements. Black, plastic roses. That drew my attention, obviously. I saw the card. I filched it."

Martha and I looked at it.

I'M GLAD YOU DIDN'T DIE. I OVERREACTED AND ALMOST MISSED THE PROPER MOMENT. PLEASE GET WELL AND FEEL IT COMPLETELY WHEN IT COMES. I WANT YOU TO KNOW THAT A DECREASE IN OXYGEN IS AN AWFUL WAY TO DIE. SLOW.

COMPLIMENTS OF THE RAGDOLL'S MAMA.

"Son-of-a-bitch," Martha said.

"Any idea when it was brought in?"

"A delivery person brought it in. Odd-looking guy, youngish, with an ugly beard and mustache. I figure now that it was fake. I didn't know what to think at the time. The cop let him in, so I assumed he was all right. He was gone, I took a peek at the card. That's when you two showed up. I slid it in my jean pocket so I could show you after you spoke with Bea."

"If they can slip in and out of the room that easy, we could just as well put a brick in the chair instead of a cop," Martha said. "Both the Pauls are behind this. They're representing Ripley's dead mother. The Ragdoll's Mama."

"No doubt," I said. "But where are they?"

⌒〜

LATE AT NIGHT, not able to sleep, I went to the bookstore and sat at the office desk and went through the stack of mail that had piled up there.

Martha had merely been heaping it onto her desk. It was an unwieldy pile. Going through it was just something to do. Also, I was looking for bills. Having water and electricity turned on was a nice service.

I had a glass of milk and the last cookie, sat and nibbled, sipped, and thought.

And then I came across a large white envelope. There was no stamp. No return address, and on the front, it simply said, DETEC-TIVE AGENCY. Obviously, it hadn't been mailed. It had been pushed through the mail slot in the door.

I opened it, wondering how long it had been lying there.

There were photographs in a stack. Six of them. I looked at them in order.

They were all of Sue Ellen, the Cassidy child. She was lying down, clutching a teddy bear. She was wearing pink pajamas with white unicorns on them. There was a leather band around her waist and it was clamped to the sides of a padded box by chains. She had leather cuffs on her wrists and ankles, and there were chains attached to the cuffs, and the opposite ends of the chains were fastened to the sides of the box like the waist strap. They were long enough to allow some movement of her wrists and ankles, but not much. She was shoeless.

The next photo was closer on her face, which was covered in sweat. If terror loans out a mask, she was wearing it.

All the shots showed her in the same position, and in each one her hair was greasy with sweat, and in the last two her eyes were closed and she looked smaller, as if she was shrinking. She had let go of the teddy bear. I was surprised the bastards had let her keep it. They had long lost touch with humanity.

The last two photos were wider shots, included part of the room she was in. I could see for sure she was in a coffin, small as a doll, and there was a large coffin lid lying on the floor next to the box. It had a smoothly bored hole near the top of one end, and there was a large piece of plastic pipe lying on the floor. I saw right away that piece of pipe would fit into the hole in the coffin lid. There was a concrete lid lying near the pipe. It too had a hole in it. Pipe through the concrete lid hole, then the coffin hole. That's how it worked.

At the end of the stack of photos was a card. Larger than the others before it. It had little sprites dancing around the edges, like a child's birthday card.

The card read: DID YOU KNOW RIPLEY DIED ON HER BIRTHDAY? DID YOU KNOW SHE WAS HUNGRY? THIRSTY? DID YOU KNOW SHE GRAD-UALLY LOST AIR AND CONSCIOUSNESS? SHE MUST HAVE CRIED FOR HER MAMA. I KNOW SUE ELLEN HAS. SHE WILL BE SENT BACK TO YOU IN TIME. WHEN YOU LEAST EXPECT IT, HER WITHERED FLESH OR STINK-ING BONES WILL ARRIVE. YOU MIGHT WANT TO PLAN THE FUNERAL. I SUGGEST A CLOSED CASKET. CREMATION WOULD BE BETTER.

The Ragdoll's Mama.

I GOT ONE of our Polaroid cameras and took photos of the photos, as well as the card, and then I called Sam and he came over with a cop in uniform. Sam looked weary and sleepy. He looked at the envelope and the photos and the card. He had a small magnifying glass he used to look at them. I didn't mention I had made photos of the photos.

"You're a regular Sherlock Holmes," I said.

"He got the brains. I got the magnifying glass. You know your fingerprints will be all over this stuff," Sam said.

"How was I to know it was evidence?"

"Still, we'll need your prints to check against others that might be on them."

"I bet there aren't any others," I said. "Ragdoll's Mama seems too clever for that."

"You have to face the fact, that with these photos lying here for a time, the child may already be dead."

"I've thought of that," I said. Then I told him about the card, and the black roses.

"The false delivery man got into the room without effort," I said. "You should put your man on higher alert. Bring someone else in. No one should go into that room, even a delivery man with flowers."

"I will do that, immediately. It's the Pauls, isn't it? They're the Ragdoll's Mama."

"We think so."

He picked up the phone and called the station. Some yelling was involved. When he hung up the phone, he said, "Why would the Ragdoll's Mama send the photos to you?"

"They know we've worked for the Cassidys, obviously. The hoax exchange in the cemetery. It's a terrorism campaign. Guess they've included us in all this as part of their crusade."

Sam was leaning over the photos with the magnifying glass.

"It's pretty obvious that the child is in a coffin and has limited air. But they did remove the lid, perhaps to let it fill up with air again, to make the vengeance last longer, and to take these photos. And if you look closely in this photo…"

He put that one in front of me.

"What am I looking at?"

"Check the top of the pipe."

He handed me the magnifying glass.

I looked at the photo through the glass. The hole in one end of the pipe was partially obstructed by something. I hadn't really noticed that before.

"It has some kind of barrier. Is that duct tape and cardboard?"

"I think so," Sam said. "Here's what I figure. Each day, or every few days, he's allowing less air to flow through the pipe. He may be opening the lid completely now and then, like here, to take a look at her. To delight in what they're doing. Allows the coffin to fill with air again, starts over. These are some seriously sick fucks, Plebin. But the trick is, where are they? Where is Sue Ellen?"

A BAND OF cops showed up, took my fingerprints and the photos, the note, and went away. I called Martha and Jasmine, and they joined me at the store. I filled them in on the photos, what Sam had pointed out.

"I have to talk to Velma again," I said.

"Oh, and last time we did, it went so well," Martha said.

"I know, but there's no choice. Sam is bound to try her again, but I think I need to beat him to it. The cops go there she might lawyer up."

"But because you're so charming and have such a great history with her," Martha said. "You feel she'll give you anything you want?"

"I think maybe my charm factor was down a notch earlier. Now, I'm feeling juiced."

EARLY NEXT MORNING, I went over to the funeral home. Luckily the doors to Velma's business were open, and I found her in her office. A teary couple were just leaving, having lost a loved one, no doubt.

When they were out of hearing, Velma said, "I hate you. You know that?"

"I know."

"You should leave. And now."

"I came to apologize."

"I don't believe that."

"Really. I did."

"But you're still looking for answers you think I have."

"I am, but not what you think. Hear me out."

I took from my coat pocket the photos I had taken of the photos of the little girl. I said, "I'm showing you something I'm not supposed to, Velma. That's because I believe you're innocent, but if you know it or not, you're connected. I don't know how, but you are."

"Oh my God," she said, looking at the photos. "Is this what I think it is? The missing little girl?"

"It is. These are copies. Cops have the originals. And you know what, that coffin, I bet it's from here. I bet that because they stole a body from here, and I think they wanted the coffin so they could bury her underground and gradually sap her air. She may already be dead, but I'm having hope she's still alive. These were in the office for a time before I discovered them. I want to ask you if that coffin came from here?"

We had been standing in the doorway of her office, but she went inside with the photos and I followed. She sat down behind her desk and took the shot with the coffin and put it front and center. She took a magnifying glass from her desk drawer, same kind Sam and

Martha had. I needed to get one. I felt left out. She studied the photo for quite a while.

"That's our Sleep Rest in Eternity model. And I will guarantee it came from here. It's a popular brand. It's cheap. They quit making them a year ago, but we bought up the last of their stock. Come with me."

She gave me back the photos and led me into the display coffin room where we had been found out the night before. There was a door off that room, and it led into another. It was storage. There were stacks of neatly arranged coffins. They all looked like the one in the photo. She took me to one spot and said, "A coffin is missing. I hadn't noticed because I wasn't really looking for it, but one's gone from this stack."

She made her way to a side door, unlocked and opened it. It led into the alley behind her business.

"They must have come in this way. But we keep it locked. Or now that Jeremy is gone, I do."

I went outside and studied the doorway. I took out my lock set, and with both of us standing in the alley, I reached inside and set the lock button and closed the door. I took out one of my tools, stuck it in the key opening, wiggled the device a little, and it snicked open.

"A chimpanzee with a nail file could get inside this door without much effort."

"You just proved that," Velma said.

"I think the killers, the kidnappers, shopped around here until they found a coffin that they could easily drill a hole into its lid to contain the air pipe. Jeremy, your assistant, probably suggested this one, as well as let them in for dope money.

"Later, they decided to take care of him, tie up loose ends, and when they did, he was dressed in his favorite outfit, dosed on heroin. To make sure he didn't talk to someone they didn't want him to talk to, they killed him. When they took the coffin, they stole your ex-husband's body. I think they thought of that on the spot. An adjustment to their plan. A body in the cemetery for hoots. Your husband was just dead in the wrong place at the wrong time."

〰

I TOLD HER about the terror campaign, went into a bit of detail. I was taking a chance telling her what I told her, but I was ready to let a starving tiger lick pork grease off my balls if it would lead to an answer.

"I understand your persistence a little better," Velma said.

"Besides a body being stolen, a coffin, could there have been anything else happening here? Something Jeremy might have done?"

"No. He did his work when he wasn't falling off the wagon." She paused. A light went on in her lovely eyes. "Well… I don't know. I can't see how it's connected."

"Well, what?"

"I needed some work done, and he suggested someone to do some construction, expand the building a little. But, that's it. Nothing weird. But he was insistent on the people he recommended."

"What about them?"

"They did a great job while they did the job. They did expand the showroom for me. Supposed to break the wall open to my office, make it larger, but then they quit showing up. I wanted my advance back. Called their number a half-dozen times, but it's not working. I called the Better Business Bureau, for what they're worth. I did find out through them that no one has a construction company at that address. I drove over there to be sure. It's a lot out in the sticks. All that's there is a little trailer."

"What did they look like?"

"The older man was bland-looking. Up close you could see he'd had some kind of facial injury, had some work done. The son was a hot little thing. Blond and beautiful."

"Twenties?"

"I'd say so. Said he worked weekends for his dad in construction, during the week he had another job. Something about him bothered me too. It was like talking to a Ken doll."

"He say what his other job was?"

"No. His father cut him off and made him get to work. Drove him hard. They were having Jeremy help them for some side pay. He knew a little about construction. Why I trusted his recommendation. Said he used to do that kind of work in the summers."

"I think the construction couple played Jeremy. Spotted right off he had a problem. Used him. He had a monkey on his back, so he was easy to play for money to feed his habit that you thought was gone, but wasn't."

"That's possible," she said.

"Do you still have the card they gave you?"

MARTHA HAD WAITED in the car while I visited with Velma. I was shit on Velma's list, but Martha, having clocked one of the clowns with her golf club, was fresher shit and fly-swarmed.

I climbed in the car and as she drove away, I told her what I had learned, the address to check out.

It was a location about twenty minutes out of town. It was a little trailer and looked damn near like a toy. It could have easily been pulled uphill in a snow storm by a Volkswagen with a flat tire. I was surprised it didn't turn over when the wind blew brisk.

The trailer was situated on the back of a lot mostly scraped to the clay. We parked on the dirt road next to some broken-up cement that might have been a parking lot about the time of the Flintstones.

We walked up to the trailer and Martha knocked with her golf club. No one answered.

Martha eased around to the window by the doorway and looked in. "Pretty neat in there, but no one seems home."

"You sure?"

"Except for inside the shitter, because the door's closed, I can see the whole damn place. He's fond of hanging things on wall hooks."

"You'd have to be, to have any kind of room at all. Okay, you or me?"

"I'm faster," Martha said, took out her lock pick and looked around. No one drove by on the narrow road. A bird flew over, its shadow coasting over the ground. It was so quiet out there you could have heard a frog fart. Martha worked the lock tools and had us inside before you could have said, "Ain't that a couple burglars?'"

There was barely room for the both us. Small enough you couldn't have kept an ant farm for pets.

I sat on the couch, which had a pillow and blankets on it, proving it to also be the bed. In fact, that one room was pretty much it. For a kitchen the owner had a set of dresser drawers with a hot

plate sitting on top, plugged in to a blacked outlet that screamed
"Someday, I'm gonna burn this motherfucker down."

There was a coffee pot sitting on a wooden chopping block next
to the hot plate, some sugar packs, and some powdered creamer.
Martha opened the dresser drawers one at a time.

"Lots of ramen noodles," she said. "You just going to sit there?"

"No room for me to move around."

"Is that a fat joke?"

"Only if you want it to be."

I got up and inched past Martha. It was such a tight squeeze I
almost ended up wearing Martha's pants as I passed. I opened a slid-
ing closet door, pulled a light string. The light was about as bright
as a candle in a pumpkin. Considering the miniature trailer, the
closet was reasonably wide and deep. There was a bar with clothes
on hangers.

"These clothes belong to a young man," I said.

I pushed aside the clothes on the bar and looked at the back wall.
"Oh hell," I said.

NEXT MOMENT, MARTHA was looking over my shoulder.

"Well," she said, "we got our guys."

"Only one person could live here," I said. "We got one guy.
Figure Traven moved out of his apartment because he knew things
were getting hot. I assume they own or rent this as a spot for their
company, which is mostly a front."

Pushing the clothes wide apart, I could see the back wall was
covered with photos and newspaper clippings. The clippings were

about the death of Ripley Paul. There were photos of the Cassidy family, relatively recent. There were photos of Sue Ellen playing in the yard with a doll house. Photos of her at school. With two people I thought might be her aunt and uncle.

On a shelf close to the floor, I found sheets of paper with numbers on them. I studied them. I couldn't make out what they meant. I handed them to Martha.

Martha said, "It's math to figure out how much air is in a coffin and how long it will last."

"No joke?"

"No joke. I did alright in algebra. And they said I'd never need it. Course, I just know that's what it is, don't ask me to crunch the numbers. I get the idea from it, though, it's about stop and start. How long it takes the coffin to refill with air, how long it takes for Sue Ellen to breathe it out. That's speculation to some degree, but basically, that's what it's about."

"Torture."

"And of a child," she said.

I fumbled around on the shelf, through more notes, found a copy of a photo cut from a newspaper. It was Mr. Paul and his son. Both gave the impression of empty paper sacks.

"I know who the man in the newspaper photo is," I said.

"Of course you do. The clipping says who it is."

"I mean I know who he is now. Where he is. So do you."

Martha leaned forward and studied the photo.

And we were rushing out of there.

The Events Concerning Two Stabbed Clowns in a Bloody Bathtub

THE NEIGHBORHOOD WAS quiet. I heard a car backfire one street over, and then there was nothing. We didn't park in front of the house we wanted, but instead parked down the street at the curb. Not that it would help much. Two people walking along the bare street, one of peculiar appearance with a golf club, was bound to be memorable. And of course, I would be remembered because I am uncontestably adorable.

"What if we're wrong?" Martha said.

"We're not. He may have changed some things, but I got to thinking how long they've planned this, the extremes they would go to, and then looking at the photo again, it all snapped together for me."

We came to the Cassidys' neighbor's house. The one that gardened and had a front-end loader. There was a blue jeep parked next to the curb in front of the house. Last time I had seen it, it was parked in from of the Cassidy business. Traven's, of course.

I was thinking how the neighbor had watched us, thinking of the description Jasmine had given us of his face. The reason for his front-end loader in the backyard. I had an idea now what he had used it for. What he had built, carefully over time, likely with his son's help.

A concrete bunker. One that would have a pit with a coffin in it, and Sue Ellen inside. The bastard had moved next to them a long time back. He watched and waited until Sue Ellen was the right age; the age his daughter had been when she died. The Cassidy couple wouldn't have recognized him, not the way his face had changed, not unless they spent a lot of time around him, and when they did finally see him up close, he had on clown makeup. So did his son, the knife-happy avenger who had grown up in the long shadow of revenge.

"I say we don't knock," I said.

Joe R. Lansdale

Martha was ahead of me. She already had her lock pick set out, and was starting to work. Right then, if I knew who had invented lock-picking, I would have sucked his dick.

The house was cool and the living room was well lit from light coming through the windows. The furniture wasn't overly expensive, but it was nice. I would have been happy to have farted in any of those chairs.

"I don't guess you brought a gun?" Martha said.

"Nope. Don't like them."

"I could like one now," she said.

We traipsed through the house, into the kitchen. There were sandwich makings on the table, plates, scraps of food. Nothing looked moldy or old; it was recent.

Checking all the rooms we found nothing.

I walked to the back door. It was mostly made of glass, framed with wood and aluminum.

I looked out at the yard. I didn't see anything but a small front-end loader. There were marks in the grass that were so deep you could tell they were tire marks from rolling machinery. They were old, but the imprints were still there. This time of year, grass was short and slow-growing. There were bare flower beds along the sides of the wooden fence, and a shed at the back. There was a small tree near the shed. The tall one that I had seen from the top of from the Cassidys' front door steps. It was bright green. It wasn't an evergreen tree. It wasn't the time of year for that sort of tree to be green.

"Martha, let's see what's out back."

We went out there, walked to the shed, the back fence. Nothing odd there. I examined the tree. Plastic leaves, and something else.

"Martha, look at this."

There was a large black plastic pipe that was the trunk of the tree. The pipe went in between plastic limbs and leaves that had been fastened to it. It was obvious now that it wasn't a tree at all.

Martha made a step with her hands and I stepped into it. That way, I could reach the top of the pipe. The mouth of it was mostly covered in cardboard and duct tape. Sue Ellen would feel like she was breathing through a soft drink straw.

I pulled out my pocket knife and cut that business loose, pulled it off and dropped it on the ground. I jumped out of Martha's hands.

"I don't know how much that helps at his point," I said, folding up my knife.

"Can't hurt, if she's still down there. If she's still alive."

The pipe tree vibrated slightly.

"They're down there," Martha said. "Moving around, near the pipe."

I nodded. If the pipe was fastened to the coffin, it was unlikely they would know we had fixed it so more air came through the pipe. But if I bumped the pipe. If they saw it move, they'd know someone was up here.

I went to the shed and started to open it, but it was locked with a key. There was one window on the side of the shed. I looked inside. Tools hung on the walls. Even a jack hammer. A lawnmower named Cleveland and a weed-eater named Herbert were visible.

I took off my shoe and beat out the window glass with three firm strikes. I reached through the gap and flipped the window latch and lifted the frame. I brushed the glass away from the sill, put my shoe on, started climbing through. One more cookie and a glass of milk that week, and I wouldn't have made it.

Once inside I flipped the inside door latch, let Martha in. The shed was bigger than Traven's trailer, but not by much. We looked around. I studied the lawnmower. It was parked in the middle of the floor. The floor looked a little weak there, like the weight of the lawnmower was dropping it slightly. I moved the mower. Where the mower had set, there was an outline of a trapdoor.

We had taken to talking quietly now.

"You should go call the cops," I said. "I'll have a look."

"And leave you to deal with this? Not likely."

I felt around the edge of the trapdoor, located an indentation I could slip my middle finger into. I took a deep breath and lifted it.

THERE WERE STAIRS that led down. Nice well-made, wooden stairs. I went down them and Martha followed, leaving the trapdoor up. That way some light slipped in.

It was stuffy as a hairy armpit in a steam room. The light from the trap faded as we went down a long hallway, narrow and dark, bleeding dampness and giving out the aroma of mildew and mold. I took out one of the tools of our trade. My penlight. I pointed it into the darkness. The beam my light gave was thin and desperate, but it was better than nothing.

Rats moved out of the darkness and along the side of the wall, and then one darted into a pool of deeper shadow on the floor and was gone.

I pointed the light. The pool of shadow was a gap in the floor. A surprise pit for invaders. We stood on the lip of the drop-off and I pointed the light down. It must have been about ten feet down and there were a half a dozen broadly spaced spikes embedded in the concrete floor.

I leapt over the pit and stood on solid ground.

"That might not be something I can do," Martha said.

"It's okay. Stay here. I'll check."

"Goddamn my bad leg," she said.

"It's all right."

"Find something to put across the gap for me."

"If I see something."

"Shit, Plebin. You're on your own."

I moved along then, watching walls and floor. I didn't find any more pits and the walls didn't close in on me and neither did a raven quote Never More.

There were tunnels to the left and the right. I chose one, and it went a short distance before ending in a pile of rubble. I went back and followed the other trail.

It went along with offshoot off trails connected to it. I decided that the initial construction was an old bomb shelter from the fifties, and that the Pauls had built out from it, expanding. Being construction workers, whatever needed to be done they could have done it easy.

What did they talk about while expanding this labyrinth? Did they talk at all? If they did, was it about a child's last breaths, the pleasure they would take in that?

I tried some of the offshoot trails, but most were unfinished and stacked at the end with rubble. Some of the short tunnels ended at small empty rooms. False starts? To be finished later?

And then there was another set of steps. The steps went down into darkness, and when I reached the bottom of them, I could see a gold light. I could hear a generator humming like a drunk blowing on a comb covered with wax paper.

I stepped on something. There was a click. Lights came on all along the hallway and they were as bright as the face of the sun.

I was light blind for an instant.

All I could see were little swimming shadows. Then I could see a larger shadow moving toward me. As my sight began to clear, I realized it was someone running at me. Instants before that someone hit me like a linebacker, my eyes became adjusted enough to see his face.

Traven.

⌇

IT WAS SUCH a hard impact my teeth snapped together and I was knocked off my feet. I rolled like a doodle bug and into the wall.

He dropped on his knees between my legs, grabbed my throat, began to choke. I lifted my right leg and put the bottom of my foot on his thigh and pushed. He slid back. I used that moment to roll him. It wasn't an easy roll, and I almost didn't manage it, but when I did, I came to my feet quickly. He made it to his feet effortlessly and kicked me in the balls. Instead of going down and out, it gave me a shot of adrenaline. I went straight at him, hit him with my head and drove him back. He clasped his forearm under my neck and rolled backwards and kicked me between the legs when he did. This time, my balls were all out of adrenaline.

I flipped over and landed on my back hard enough to lose my breath. He was straddling me again. I took two shots before I realized I was being hit. It hurt.

There was a whistling sound, a glint of silver from the wall lights, and the shiny end of Martha's putter clipped Traven hard enough on the side of his chin I saw his jaw actually move from left to right. He tumbled off of me and his feet went up against the wall.

An open hand shot down at me.

I took Martha's hand and she helped me up.

"I decided bad knee or not, I was going to get over that gap," she said. "Nearly fell in, but managed."

"I'm glad you did."

On my feet again, we cautiously slipped along the tunnel and into greater light. It was the room in the photos, but now we could see more of it. There were photos on the wall. I assumed they were of Ripley Paul. A beautiful girl. There was even one of her in her ragdoll Halloween costume, obviously taken right before she went out to trick-or-treat and was struck by the car Bea was driving. Hanging next to that photo on a peg was a child's ragdoll outfit, dirty and blood-stained.

There was a small TV and the only thing on the screen was a bit of light in a dark box. In the box—coffin to be exact—was Sue Ellen—a scrap of a child with matted hair covering most of her face. The chains were still in place, ending in cuffs fastened to her wrists and ankles. The light was from the hole in the air pipe.

I saw the spot where the coffin would be in the floor. I recognized it from the photos. The pipe, the false tree, ran up from the floor and through a gap in the roof. There was a looped pull rope fastened into the concrete lid. I trembled and started for it.

Then the lights went out. The darkness was as complete as the final crack of Doom.

I HEARD A grunt and then a sound like someone dropping two hundred pounds of potatoes on a rock, and something fell across my feet.

That would be Martha, I thought. I ducked low and something whistled over my head. I sensed it had come from behind, so I pulled my captured feet out from under Martha, turned, still staying low, reached out and got hold of cloth.

Pants legs.

I drove forward, my head between the pants legs, lifted my head and shoulders and raised the pants owner up. I threw my arms high and arched my back, heard a disagreeable snapping sound and an expulsion of air that could easily have been confused for a long-held fart by the wearied universe.

I managed to turn, and as if by radar, I found the body. I jumped on top of it and started pounding, burying my fists in flesh. But my opponent wasn't moving. That crack on the head had put him out. We were all getting our heads cracked this night.

I had lost my penlight, so I felt around until I could touch Martha. I felt something damp on the palm of my hand.

The back of Martha's skull. She had taken one hard as hell lick.

"Get the girl," Martha said. It had taken a lot of will power for her to say that.

"I need your penlight," I said.

"Coat pocket."

I patted around trying to find it.

"Goddamn it," Martha said, and I heard her sit up with the effort of a dying elephant. "Guess, wounded as I am, I have to do it myself. Maybe I should fix you a little supper while we're here."

She pulled the penlight out of her pocket, flipped it on. It wasn't much but it punched a little hole in the dark.

Martha had lost her wool hat. It was beside her. She took hold of it and slipped it on. I helped her up and we hustled to where the pipe ran up from the floor.

I pulled the pipe up, and pushed the bottom portion to the side. I leaned down and got hold of the pull rope. The concrete lid screeched as I pulled. It was heavy. I swung it off to the side. I put my hand in the hole in the coffin where the pipe had fit, and pulled up on it.

And there in Martha's penlight glow was Sue Ellen.

MARTHA FOUND A switch and turned it on. The generator hummed.

Martha came back and used her lock pick on Sue Ellen's cuffs. We had the kid loose in no time. I lifted her gently out of the coffin. I thought, ironically, she felt like a ragdoll in my arms. She smelled awful; a stench of sweat and urine and feces and fear.

I laid her out on a rug on the floor and put my head to her chest. Her heart was beating, but it sounded faint. She was breathing poorly, and then she wasn't. She started gulping air, but didn't come awake.

I let her breathe deep, hoping that would do the trick for her. I turned and looked around. Lying on the floor next to a two-by-four he had used to hit Martha was Mr. Paul. Or the man who had formerly been known by that name. I went over and looked at him. His face had had some work. It was mostly without wrinkles. Dead looking. His toupee was twisted on his head from the impact of his fall. His mouth was open. His false teeth were crooked. His caterpillar mustache seemed firm, however.

"I'm going to kill him with that two-by-four," Martha said.

"No, Martha. No killings. Come help me with the kid."

We heard a noise then, a pounding of shoe leather going away from us. Traven had awakened and was making his exit along the tunnel. To hell with his father. Traven had thrown in the towel.

"Let him go," I said.

"Like I'm up to chasing him." Martha had sat down in a chair and had a hand pressed to the back of her head. "I'm nauseous. I can't be of much help."

We heard a loud scream and a loud smacking sound, and then silence.

"What the hell?" I said.

"I have an idea," Martha said.

There was a little refrigerator in the room, and I looked inside and found a bottle of water, and used that to gently wet Sue Ellen's lips. I sprinkled a little on her face. She managed to open her eyes.

"It's okay, baby," I said. "We're taking you home."

I cut the cord off a lamp, then one off of a small, rotating fan, and used those to tie up Paul of the wayward toupee. He didn't fight it. He didn't do anything.

"I'll help you get the kid across the hole in the floor, then I'll come back and lay on the floor for a nap while you carry her out, and call the police. Tell them an ambulance would be nice. Ask if they provide snacks."

I carried Sue Ellen in my arms, Martha trailing behind me, using the golf club as a cane. When we came to the hole in the floor, I noticed in the beam from the penlight Martha was holding that the floor was damp.

"I peed there," she said.

Then she poked the light into the hole. There was Traven, like a collapsed puppet. He groaned when Martha moved the light around but didn't move much. There was a spike poking through one leg and his left shoulder. Miraculously, the others had missed him.

"You see," she said, "I managed over that hole by falling forward and then sort of tugging myself over, my feet dangling for a while. When I got up on this side, I was overcome with the need to pee. So, I dropped trousers and peed. Traven came here, running in the dark, stepped in it, slid right into the hole."

"A fortuitous wee-wee," I said.

There's not a lot more to tell after that. We got Sue Ellen over the hole in the floor by me hopping over, then leaning forward as Martha sort of pushed her at me. I got Sue Ellen and pulled her over and Martha leaned forward and puked into the hole, onto Traven. Then she tossed me the penlight, eased against the wall and slid down it into a sitting position.

"I think I'm going to black out," she said, and promptly did.

I went out of there with Sue Ellen and placed her in a big stuffed chair and made a call on the kitchen phone. The cops and a couple of ambulances came in short time. One took Sue Ellen away, and after some directions and warnings from me about the pit, they fetched Martha and put her in the other ambulance and hauled her away.

There were some uniform cops of course. Harry Johnson, Butch and Sam were with them. I had asked for Sam, and that caused them all to come. They interrogated me in the living room. I lay on the couch. I wasn't feeling so good myself by then. I had been banged up good in my tussle with Traven.

They left Traven in the hole for a while until one of the ambulances came back, without sirens, driving slowly. No one seemed in a hurry now. That suited me, goddamn child torturers. I didn't care if he bled to death.

Bad Plebin, but there you have it.

I turned my head as I lay on the couch, watched as Traven and his father were hauled out, bringing them through the house. The father, on his cot, opened his eyes and looked at me as they toted him by.

"I won't forget you," he said.

"Thank you," I said. "As for you, you're already forgotten."

This wasn't true, of course, but it sounded tough.

Sam, Butch and Harry Johnson—I always thought of him with full name—were still gathered around where I lay on the couch.

Sam said, "You just had to put the police to shame again. Couldn't call and tell us where the girl was."

"Wasn't positive we were right, and there was no time to waste," I said.

"Sure, that makes it all right," Harry Johnson said, but I thought he sounded as if he actually meant it.

⌒

I GUESS THIS is what you call the wrap-up.

A bit of close-out information on the Events Concerning the Ragdoll's Mama, as we named the case, then filed it away in our file drawer.

Traven's fall into the pit, the spikes, didn't do him any good, to say the least. His spine is jacked, so he spends a lot of time in a prison hospital watching football and receiving mental health care. Or so I've heard. It's not like he's getting a visit from me.

The Events Concerning Two Stabbed Clowns in a Bloody Bathtub

Mr. Paul, or Andy as he called himself—ah Raggedy Andy, just got it—the ragdoll's daddy and representative for Ripley's mother's, found a way to hang himself in custody. Sheets and window cell bars; a classic. He went right to it, still wearing bandages on his head where my throw had cracked his skull.

I'd rather have seen him get the death penalty. I'm not usually that way, but I'd have gone to see that execution and had a big meal afterwards, took a happy shit and slept like a baby.

Sue Ellen, she recovered, and so did her mother. Dark shadows will move between those two for a while. Father's dead. And a bad crime in Bea's past led to her daughter's situation and the death of her husband. Even though we hadn't been officially still on the case, Bea paid us a lot. I turned it down, but Martha didn't. Good thing. Now we have enough money to do us for a while. Maybe I will consider a down payment on a house.

I also figured out the last name Traven was using on his name plaque in the accounting office was karma spelled backwards. Just thought you might like to know.

Martha got better quick. She's tough as the proverbial boot. She's might even be a bigger asshole now than she was before.

Jasmine, thank goodness, quit seeing Butch and has gone back to school. She's taking courses in criminology. I wonder how long that will stick. At least she hasn't stopped baking cookies. I like that hangover from her would-be baker days.

I don't care where she ends up job wise as long as she's happy. But I hope she passes on the recipe for those cookies to me, if she should decide to stop baking them. Giving it to Martha would be a disaster. She can't boil water with a cook book and help from a personal assistant.

Joe R. Lansdale

Me, I'm back on cases involving skulking around and taking photos of cheating spouses and reading books I buy or lift from the bookstore. I thought for a while I might try to patch up things with Velma, go for that coffee. But there's that whole clown and orgy business between us. I'm not hip enough for that shit. Also, as Martha said, I have coffee at the bookstore.

I like the bookstore. I like the detective agency. I've finally come to that conclusion.

Guess it's not such a bad life.

Still, there are some scars.

Sometimes at night, I imagine myself down in that dark hole with the pipe sticking through the top of the coffin, my arms and ankles clamped to the sides of the box, trying hard to take a good, clean breath.

That's when I awake with my chest heaving and in a cold sweat.